"You're te_____ Josh. "You don't seem to have much sympathy for poor Sandy."

"Well, I told her I still wanted to be friends."

"That's the oldest line in the book! No woman falls for that."

Josh looked at Peter—his best friend and JoJo's boyfriend. "I think she's on to us, bud."

"I think you're right," Peter said. "We men of the nineties need to come up with some new lines."

JoJo sighed. She knew *Peter* would never really use that line. He was so nice...so levelheaded. Through all their time together he'd been her Rock of Gibraltar.

Trouble was, rocks weren't always so romantic....

Dear Reader,

Okay, you have a boyfriend...and you've had him for quite a while. The rosy glow of those first moments together has turned into long moments in front of the bluish glow of the TV set. What do you do when those hot dates turn into, well, somewhat lukewarm rent-the-video-and-order-the-pizza moments? Do you hit the lingerie section of the store? Or do you get going?

It happens to the best of us. And in this episode of THE LOOP it happens to JoJo. I mean, not everyone is so marriage obsessed as C.J.'s been—*some* people actually want to look around before they settle down....

So what's a gal to do? Read and find out....

Lucia Macro

Senior Editor
Silhouette Books

Please address questions and book requests to:
Silhouette Reader Service
U.S.: 3010 Walden Ave., P.O. Box 1325, Buffalo, NY 14269
Canadian: P.O. Box 609, Fort Erie, Ont. L2A 5X3

Getting Away With It: JoJo

LIZ IRELAND

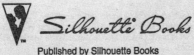

Published by Silhouette Books
America's Publisher of Contemporary Romance

If you purchased this book without a cover you should be aware that this book is stolen property. It was reported as "unsold and destroyed" to the publisher, and neither the author nor the publisher has received any payment for this "stripped book."

 SILHOUETTE BOOKS

ISBN 0-373-20208-3

GETTING AWAY WITH IT: JOJO

Copyright © 1995 by Harlequin Enterprises B.V.

All rights reserved. Except for use in any review, the reproduction or utilization of this work in whole or in part in any form by any electronic, mechanical or other means, now known or hereafter invented, including xerography, photocopying and recording, or in any information storage or retrieval system, is forbidden without the written permission of the editorial office, Silhouette Books, 300 East 42nd Street, New York, NY 10017 U.S.A.

All characters in this book have no existence outside the imagination of the author and have no relation whatsoever to anyone bearing the same name or names. They are not even distantly inspired by any individual known or unknown to the author, and all incidents are pure invention.

This edition published by arrangement with Harlequin Enterprises B.V.

SASSY is a registered trademark of Sassy Publishers, Inc., used with permission.

® and TM are trademarks of Harlequin Enterprises B.V., used under license. Trademarks indicated with ® are registered in the United States Patent and Trademark Office, the Canadian Trade Marks Office and in other countries.

Printed in U.S.A.

WHO'S WHO

JOJO GIAMETTI:
What was she *doing* with Peter anyway? She was an actress, not a future housewife. (Okay, she wasn't an actress, she was a temp...but she certainly wasn't a *bore.*) Peter was so reliable, so stable...so dull. And if she spent one more holiday with his wholesome family arguing over who got the biggest slice of pumpkin pie, she was going to scream!

PETER LATTIMORE:
All right, he wasn't Mr. Spontaneity—but what had he done to make JoJo reject him? Drink too much milk? Get eight hours of sleep? Have a real job? He'd stay up all night with a beer in his hand if that would make her happy...but she'd known when she met him he wasn't like that.

JOSH BAXTER:
Knew he was God's gift to womankind. And now that JoJo was having problems with Peter, he could move right in on her. Trouble was, would he want to keep her once he got her?

For my wonderful agent, Alice Orr.

One

Those blue eyes spelled trouble. JoJo Giamatti couldn't be sure what Josh was up to, but he was looking at her in that strange way again, just as he had since she'd come over to his and Peter's apartment late that afternoon. Just as she'd noticed him looking at her for the past few weeks, as a matter of fact. His eyes were dark blue and shone with equal parts mischief and what seemed to be flirtation.

But that was impossible, JoJo thought. She was his best friend's girlfriend. She forced her attention back to the television, where Peter's favorite show, "Sixty Minutes," was in full swing.

"Aren't you glad nosy news reporters don't run the world?" Josh asked after a moment.

He wasn't talking to anyone in particular, but JoJo and Peter both looked up from the couch, where they were sprawled in typical Sunday-night vegetative position. On-screen, Mike Wallace was at his pushy reporter best, knocking on the door of a shady business. As usual, no one was answering.

"Are you insulting my show again?" Peter asked. "I like Mike Wallace."

"The man doesn't let anybody get away with anything! He's like Big Brother—with really high Neilsen ratings."

JoJo laughed. "Josh, you're paranoid."

His blue eyes widened defensively and he pointed an accusing finger at the tube. "That's because Peter's turning on stuff like this all the time. Why do we watch this program, anyway?"

Peter sat up like a shot, dislodging JoJo from his chest. "Hey, this is high-quality programming!"

JoJo lay back on the couch with one eye on the television, listening to Josh and Peter banter back and forth about each other's choice of TV shows. Maybe that was what those blue eyes had been twinkling about; Josh had been gearing up for one of their usual good-natured debates. Josh liked movies and music videos, and Peter was addicted to news shows. How these two had managed to be friends since kindergarten was beyond her comprehension.

Maybe it was because they were such opposites that their friendship had been so long-lived. Peter, her boyfriend for almost two years now, was a real guy's guy. He liked the Chicago Bears, rock and roll, and greasy hamburgers. Josh, on the other hand, prided himself on being a lady's man, on his eclectic tastes and a prowess in the kitchen that would make the Frugal Gourmet green with envy.

Peter and Josh looked nothing alike, either. Josh was taller and thinner, had dark hair that was more often long than not and dressed with a flair that spoke of his love of anything foreign—bright Indian prints, spiffy Italian shoes, a bush hat his eccentric mother had brought back from Australia. Tonight he was simply in jeans and a long-sleeved T-shirt with a grunge-band logo on it, but he still looked as if he had stepped off the pages of a magazine.

Peter also wore jeans, but with a red-and-black-flannel shirt neatly tucked in. There was nothing flashy about him, yet he had a certain clean-cut American kid charm that JoJo found adorable. He always dressed conservatively, right down to the round wire frames on his glasses. His blond hair was worn in a plain, short and simple cut; to have it any other way would have raised eyebrows at the stodgy office where he worked as an accountant, and Peter didn't like to make waves. Not for superficial reasons, at least. On matters of principle he could be tenacious and argumentative, but how people dressed or wore their hair didn't interest him much.

Lately he hadn't even seemed to have noticed how *she* looked. Tonight, for instance, JoJo had worn a cool new angora sweater and matching skirt that she'd found in a boutique by her mom's house in the 'burbs, and Peter hadn't said a word. Josh had spotted the clothes the minute she came through the door. Of course, he had told her she looked like a newly sheared sheep—but the way his eyes had lingered over her figure had let her know in a very direct way that he'd only been teasing.

Peter and Josh were like oil and water, yet they had managed, without killing each other—so far—to share a modest two-bedroom apartment in Chicago since leaving the University of Iowa two years ago.

"I like this show," JoJo put in before the two of them ruined a perfectly good friendship over something so totally stupid as "Sixty Minutes." Though, if she were forced to tell the truth, she would rather be watching a movie, too. She didn't have cable at her apartment, so there wasn't much to see on her television except snow.

"There. You see?" Peter said smugly.

Josh looked at her with those killer blue eyes of his and winked. "Traitor."

"She's *my* girlfriend," Peter said.

"Besides, I think Mike Wallace is kind of cute," JoJo added, for shock value as much as anything else.

"Oh, yuck!" Josh and Peter cried in unison.

"JoJo, the man has to be seventy if he's a day," Peter said.

She shrugged as the phone rang. "Okay, so he's cute in a grandfatherly way."

The phone rang again and Josh unfolded himself from his chair to get it. He leaned against the counter that separated the living room from the small narrow kitchen and sent JoJo another of those half-flirtatious looks of his. "I'm glad to hear you haven't started going in for older guys," he said.

Those eyes. Everywhere JoJo turned tonight, she seemed to find herself staring into them. Josh had sexy blue eyes like Tom Cruise, only Josh's were more intense, and apparently she was as vulnerable to them as the next woman. Funny she'd never noticed before.

Or maybe she had, and she just hadn't been paying attention. But lately she'd caught herself watching Peter's roommate more and more when she was over—which was practically all the time.

"Oh, Sandy, hi." Josh's expression was panicked and he gripped the phone with white knuckles. He rolled his eyes toward the ceiling, letting on that he was clearly not glad to hear from this person. Then, lowering his voice, he turned a little more toward the kitchen for privacy.

JoJo couldn't contain her curiosity. "Who's Sandy?" she asked Peter.

"A girl." He popped a piece of popcorn into his mouth and looked away from the car commercial on the screen.

"You mean a girl*friend?*" she asked.

Peter shook his head in exasperation. "One of the many." Josh had gone through more girls than Warren Beatty and, judging from the sound of his one-sided conversation, this Sandy person was putting his feet to the fire for having stood her up.

"Sandy, I'm sorry, okay?" he pleaded. JoJo and Peter were both listening intently now, and Josh sent a beleaguered shrug toward his audience. "It's just this weekend was so crazy, and I've got classes..."

Peter made a *tsk*ing sound. "Excuses, excuses."

"Watch it, Josh, or that girl's going to send Mike Wallace to bang down your door to expose your lies," JoJo joked.

"Will you two shut up?" Josh hissed with his hand over the receiver. He returned to Sandy, who was obviously still chewing him out on the other line. "No, there's no girl here, Sandy—it's the television."

Peter and JoJo nearly buckled over, laughing.

Josh frowned. "No, I *haven't* been trying to avoid you," he soothed.

"Yeah, right," Peter said. "He just happened to miss the fifty messages she's left on the machine at all hours of the day and night."

JoJo rolled her eyes as Josh threw them another despairing glance. Oddly, she felt almost nervous about what the outcome would be. Would he ask Sandy out again? She found herself hoping he wouldn't.

But why should she care? She barely knew Josh, other than as someone to make small talk with during commercials and over pizza when she was at the apartment visiting Peter.

Josh's eyes again met JoJo's and held them for a few moments. Suddenly, as she watched, an idea seemed to occur to him, something he'd figured out precisely by gazing at her.

"Sandy, I didn't want to have to tell you this..." Josh began. There was a pause as Sandy, JoJo was sure, let out a few exclamations of dread. Finally he continued, still looking straight at JoJo. "It's just...I met up with an old friend...." There was a pause, and his blue eyes darkened. "Yes, a girlfriend," he explained.

Sandy apparently had a conniption fit on the other end.

Peter shook his head. "What a liar!"

But JoJo was still too mesmerized watching Josh to say anything.

"Sandy, I can't tell you that." There was another short pause, then, still watching JoJo, Josh said, "All right. Her name's JoJo."

"What?" The words jolted JoJo to an upright sitting position.

"Hey—!" Peter sputtered his disapproval.

JoJo felt a little shiver go through her. It seemed so odd hearing him use her name like that. She and Josh hadn't been college friends at all—they'd met through Peter after she'd temped for a week at Peter's office here in Chicago. And she and Josh had certainly never gone out, never even considered it. How could they, when she was the steady girlfriend of his best and oldest friend?

Where had he gotten the idea to use her name in the lie?

Of course, he hadn't really *meant* anything by it, she assured herself as she listened to Josh hand Sandy a line about how much he valued Sandy's friendship. He'd just said her name because she was sitting there, looking at him.

But was she crazy, or had he been looking at her differently lately? And why had she started feeling so weird when their gazes happened to meet, or when they accidently bumped against each other maneuvering around the little apartment?

Finally Josh clunked down the receiver and let out a relieved rush of breath. "Phew! What a dragon."

"I thought you *liked* Sandy," Peter said.

"I did—for a few weeks." Josh shot his friend a wicked grin.

Peter shook his head. "I can't believe you just lied to her like that."

"Hey, she wouldn't let up. I completely forgot that I told her I'd call her this weekend."

"So why didn't you tell her the truth?" Peter asked, incredulous. "You didn't run into an old flame, you've been sitting at home watching television."

"I couldn't tell Sandy that."

"Why not?" Peter asked.

"Because it wouldn't have been very flattering to say I preferred television to her," Josh said.

Peter's eyebrows shot up quizzically. "And being dumped for another woman is?"

"Cool your jets, bud. It's not as though we had anything very heavy going on," Josh said. "I only met her a month ago."

"Josh is right," JoJo said. She couldn't believe she was defending Josh for dumping on poor Sandy, but she understood why he had said what he did. And maybe, she thought, she just felt like taking Josh's side.

"See?" Josh said. "My lie even gets the women's vote."

Peter sent JoJo a surprised glance. "I can't believe you're defending him. He even made you an accessory!"

JoJo laughed, but felt herself flush a little. She tried to avoid looking at Josh. "But if he had told Sandy that he'd rather spend his weekend watching cable than going out with her, that would have hurt her feelings even more."

"Even more than his finding a new girlfriend would have?" Peter asked skeptically.

"What would you think if JoJo told you that she'd rather stay at home reading than go out with you?" Josh asked him.

"I'd think she found a good book to read," Peter said matter-of-factly.

JoJo laughed again. Practical Peter *would* have an attitude like that. That was part of what she loved about him; the guy was completely unflappable. "I'm glad you think so highly of my powers of attraction, Peter. I think some people might be a little more suspicious, though," she explained.

"Oh...I didn't mean to say that you *might* not have found somebody else to go out with." Peter thought for a moment. "But I still say it's better to tell the truth."

"Even at the expense of hurting someone's feelings?" Josh asked.

"How can people communicate if they're always lying to one another?"

JoJo frowned in thought. "But people are always lying, in a way. It's just our way of being polite."

"That's right!" Josh said, jumping in. "If we didn't have little white lies, everybody would be getting ticked off at each other all the time. Society would be total chaos."

"Leave it to you to rationalize lying to your girlfriend as a theory of civilization," Peter said with mock scorn.

"Telling someone that you just decided that you would rather not go out with them, for no reason at all, just seems too cruel, Peter," JoJo said.

"Then give her a reason," Peter answered, turning to Josh. "Why don't you want to go out with Sandy anymore?"

"I don't know." Josh shrugged. "She's just so...dull."

Peter's face brightened. "Then there's your reason."

"You want me to call Sandy up and tell her she's dull?" Josh asked, flabbergasted.

"Peter!" JoJo said in amazement.

"At least that way you wouldn't be leaving her in the dark."

"No, he'd be leaving her suicidal," JoJo said. "I can't believe you would do something like that, Peter. I hope we never break up—I don't think I'd want to hear the truth about myself put that bluntly!"

Peter took her hand and squeezed it. "Okay, we'll just never break up." He leaned over and kissed her cheek.

JoJo could feel a blush creeping into her cheeks in the silence that followed. For a brief moment, her gaze met

Josh's, and then they both looked away. Why did she feel so uncomfortable? Peter had kissed her in front of Josh a million times before.

"Besides," Peter went on, oblivious to her discomfort, "I would never have anything negative to say about you. You're perfect."

"Oh, please!" JoJo protested. She pulled her hand away and pretended to be momentarily fascinated with whatever was on the television. She almost felt guilty. But for what?

"JoJo may be perfect, but Sandy's not," Josh said. "That's the problem."

"Then you should find yourself a JoJo," Peter instructed his friend. "But until then, you should tell the truth to women instead of lying to them."

Josh stood at mock Boy Scout attention. "Okay, Mr. Ethics, I'll give it a try," he said with a salute.

JoJo laughed. "Peter Ethics...I like that. It suits you better than Lattimore."

"Doesn't it?" Josh said wistfully. "It's so truthful sounding."

"Okay, okay," Peter said, smiling.

"Or how about Peter Straight Arrow?"

"That works, too," JoJo agreed.

"Peter Pencil Pusher," Josh threw out.

"Wasn't there a nursery rhyme about him? Or was that Peter Pumpkin Eater?"

"You guys are a regular laugh riot," Peter said. "What did I do to deserve such loyal, caring friends?"

With a good-natured pout on his face, Peter was irresistible. JoJo put her arms around him and gave him a big hug. "You just put up with us. That's all we require."

"Speak for yourself," Josh told her. "I also require him to help me with my taxes every April."

The three of them laughed and got back to the serious business of watching television. Unfortunately, the end credits were rolling on "Sixty Minutes."

"Oh, look!" Peter said. "It's over."

"Sorry, bud," Josh said with grave humility. "I guess if I had told Sandy the truth, you wouldn't have missed your program."

Josh sometimes joked that Peter would turn into Ward Cleaver if he didn't watch out, and now Peter took on the somber moral tone of the father from "Leave It to Beaver." "I'm glad to hear that, pal," he said with a kind but grim cast to his lips. "Maybe next time you'll know to be more considerate of others."

"You two are terrible," JoJo scolded, deciding to make a belated stand for womankind. "Neither one of you seems to have much sympathy for poor Sandy."

"I do so," Peter objected.

"Me, too," Josh said. "Besides, I told her I still wanted to be her friend."

JoJo scoffed. "That's the oldest dump line in the book! No woman falls for that."

Peter and Josh looked at each other, feigning perplexed wonder at this new tidbit about the opposite sex.

"They're on to us, bud," Josh said.

"I think you're right, pal," Peter answered. "We men of the nineties need to come up with some new lines."

JoJo ran a hand through her thick curly black hair in exasperation. "There's no arguing with you two when you get started with your 'bud and pal' routine."

Peter put his hand over hers. "You feel left out, don't you?" he asked with overdone concern.

"Hey, Pete," Josh said. "If I'm pal and you're bud, what could we call JoJo?"

They both thought for a moment, tapping their foreheads in mock concentration. "I know!" Peter said. "How about pud?"

"How about changing the channel?" JoJo suggested.

The usual brief tussle ensued. Josh won control of the remote and began flipping from station to station. With the old camaraderie between them restored, they sat in front of MTV for a little while before settling on a movie. And even though JoJo knew Peter didn't care too much for music videos or the old movie Josh chose to watch, he didn't kick up a fuss.

It was because Peter was so easygoing that she liked him so much, JoJo reminded herself. What other guy would fall for a crazy person like herself and call her perfect? She wasn't even close to perfect. She was always either worried about her fledgling acting career and making enough money to scratch by or having problems with her family. Through all of this, levelheaded Peter was her Rock of Gibraltar.

Rocks weren't always so romantic, though, a little voice inside her head whispered.

Her gaze strayed from the TV screen over to Josh's profile. The guy was undeniably good-looking. And he was funny, too. And talented. Josh would probably become a chef at a big restaurant someday, write a book and become rich and famous. At least, that was what he wanted, and JoJo, with her own dreams of an acting career, could understand his goals.

Josh looked over at her and she darted her eyes back to the television. She couldn't believe how weird she was being! Here she was, lying against one guy and mooning over another one. Peter's best friend, of all people!

Peter's best friend, who, she reminded herself sternly, had just dumped a nice girl right before her eyes. Josh was a bounder, and always had been. Peter had told her that in college Josh had been a regular campus Casanova.

That was hardly what she was attracted to in a man. Peter, on the other hand, was caring and dependable. He would never treat her the way Josh treated women, she thought with a smug zip of satisfaction. Peter was a gem.

So why couldn't she keep her eyes off Josh?

Two

By morning, as she sat on a kitchen stool sipping the coffee Peter had made her, JoJo had it all figured out. The reason why she'd been noticing Josh so much lately was because she was nostalgic for that crazy-in-love feeling she'd had with Peter in the beginning.

She'd met him over a year and a half earlier, when she'd been doing a boring receptionist temp job. Right after she'd situated herself in front of the new switchboard, the elevators had opened and there stood Peter. She remembered the way he had looked at her that first time, his big brown eyes widening beneath his glasses when he spotted her sitting behind the desk. It was love at first sight, pure and simple. Bells went off, lightning struck and an invisible force of attraction drew Peter to the desk to ask her name and when she took her coffee breaks.

By midmorning, JoJo had talked with him twice on the phone and shared an intimate coffee break chat with him. After lunch, which they had taken together, she had realized Peter knew more about her than her own mother probably did. And by the end of the day, after he'd had roses delivered to the office and secured a dinner date for that evening, she had been fairly certain she'd found the man of her dreams.

The strange thing was, he wasn't at all like the men she'd been dreaming of. All these years, the ideal man she'd conjured up in her mind had been an artistic free spirit, a combination of all the movie stars, writers and college professors she'd ever had crushes on. Her dream man had had a moody, fiery personality, yet was sensitive and caring; he'd sported clothes with dramatic holes in them and long hair he wore in a ponytail. He was not a man Mrs. Giamatti would want sitting at her dinner table on Sunday afternoons.

Unfortunately, JoJo's search for this elusive dream man had unearthed some real losers. All the men she'd dated in college had been flaky drama types, either too egotistical or too emotionally fragile for her to put up with for long. And during her two months out in the real world, she'd met mostly office drips and gropers who hung out at bars. She'd almost given up hope of finding her dream man.

Then she'd met Peter and realized that her mental image of Mr. Right for all these years had been totally, completely, one-hundred-percent wrong. But how could she have guessed that the man for her would turn out to be a clean-cut yuppie type who wore glasses and worked in accounting?

Who could predict these things?

She'd also been amazed to find out that she hadn't even been Peter's type, either. He'd had one steady girlfriend all through high school—a delicate blonde named Paige, who had been salutatorian to Peter's valedictorian. Then, at the University of Iowa, he'd found a Paige replica whom he stayed with for three years, until she went off to do graduate studies at the Sorbonne in Paris. After graduation, Peter had moved to Chicago.

And met an Italian-American fledgling actress with long frizzy black hair and a big mouth, JoJo thought with a laugh. The poor guy probably hadn't known what hit him when he stepped off that elevator. With her ample bust and dark olive complexion she was hardly a delicate waif type. More like a trimmed-down Rosie O'Donnell. And though she had done well in college, no one had ever accused her of being an Einstein.

Nevertheless, after a week of dating Peter she'd sensed she was involved in the most serious relationship of her life. She and Peter shared a love of the Chicago Bears, baseball, fast-paced bestsellers and long, leisurely walks through the city. Both wanted to get married someday and have kids—Peter, because he loved his big, perfect family, and JoJo, because she wanted to have the kind of big, perfect family her parents had aspired to before they divorced.

During those first months, it hadn't mattered at all that while Peter liked solid established rockers like the Rolling Stones, JoJo leaned toward the Crash Test Dummies and the Cranberries. She didn't think twice when he balked at going to the opera, either; what man didn't? Those things were superficial differences. The most important thing back then had been that Peter cared about her, and she had been wild to discover everything there was to know about him.

Maybe that was her problem. Nearly two years later, what else was there to discover? She was just getting a little restless, and naturally her eye was straying. It happened all the time.

But that didn't make it any less disturbing.

She felt horrible. Peter had been so nice to her this morning, even though she hadn't been very affectionate last night and he had clearly been in the mood. What was the matter with her? She usually loved it when Peter felt like cuddling. But somehow, she hadn't been able to work up the enthusiasm.

She hadn't been able to get Josh's blue eyes out of her mind, either. That was why she felt like a louse.

Had her disinterest even registered with Peter? He'd seemed so wrapped up in work lately, she wasn't sure he noticed her moods any more than her clothes. Lately, he had been so obsessed with working his way up in his company—the same one he'd been at when they'd met—that he hardly ever wanted to go out at night anymore, and after working half days on Saturdays, his weekends consisted of resting and hanging around the apartment.

"Good morning."

The sound of Josh's voice startled JoJo so much that she nearly fell off her stool. "Good morning," she said, bracing one hand against the counter in front of her. She looked purposefully into those sexy blue eyes, just to get it over with. Then her gaze traveled down. He wore black jeans and an African print shirt, unbuttoned, which revealed the muscled smoothness of his chest. There was no denying it. Josh had a great body.

She found herself looking longer than she had intended to. Josh smiled at her. "What's up?" he asked.

"Oh, I'm waiting for my temp agency to call with an assignment," JoJo said, gathering her wits. "I hope it doesn't bug you that I sometimes give them this number."

"That's okay with me."

"There's coffee. Peter made it." She was always surprised at how chipper Josh was in the morning. Peter wasn't cranky, but he definitely was slower moving; of course, he also got up earlier to go to work. He'd left the house more than an hour ago.

Josh took a sip of coffee, opened the refrigerator door and stared inside. "I think I feel like eating today."

JoJo laughed. "That's something I feel like doing every day. Of course, that's probably why this skirt feels so tight."

Josh leaned across the counter toward her and took his time giving her a long assessing stare that made her feel as if her insides were about to melt. "I don't know about your skirt, but the rest of you looks great."

JoJo glanced quickly into her coffee cup and called herself an idiot for the blush she could feel creeping into her cheeks. Josh probably thought she'd been fishing for a compliment.

"I mean it," he said, as if he could read her mind. "That burgundy color looks great on you."

She wore a silk shirt and a black wool skirt that came above her knee. "These are my office clothes. They're practically all I own that didn't come off the rack of some vintage clothing store. Unfortunately, I can't make my hair look normal to match."

Josh laughed as he looked at her cascade of black curls. "You've got terrific hair."

"It's a mop," she said good-naturedly, running her hand through a long strand.

Josh looked at his watch. "Hey, isn't it a little late for your agency not to have called?"

It was almost nine-thirty. "They do usually call before nine, but I never consider myself off the hook until ten-thirty."

"Have you eaten?" he asked.

"No, I watched Peter eat his cornflakes."

Josh's mouth curled in disgust. "Ruined your appetite, huh?"

"You're a food snob."

One jet-black eyebrow arched into his forehead. "Of course. That's why I'm spending my stepfather's hard-earned money to become a chef."

JoJo laughed. "Anyway, I usually just drink coffee in the morning."

"Then you're not really living. I'm going to make an omelette that will give you a whole new perspective on the word *breakfast.*"

How could she resist? Josh was the best cook in the world. Besides, she told herself, chances were her agency would call before the eggs were even ready. Even though she temped—ostensibly to give her time to work on her acting career—she had a reputation for being competent, and she worked pretty steadily. It was a rare day when she found herself idle.

"I've got a whole day off today," Josh said as he chopped vegetables. "It's a great feeling not to have class Mondays until six-thirty."

JoJo nodded. "I always love having time off, but I never use it the way I'm supposed to. I always find myself writing letters or zoning out in front of "Oprah" instead of practicing monologues, trying to get myself out there."

By "out there," she meant Chicago's thriving theatrical community, which was right behind New York and Los Angeles in difficulty for a newcomer trying to get her foot in the door. She had been in town for two years and had gone out on a little more than a dozen auditions in that time. There were so many talented people in the city, it was daunting. After a spate of disappointing auditions a year and a half ago, she'd stopped going on them.

At the time, she'd been so wrapped up in her relationship with Peter, she hadn't cared that she was putting her career on hold. Lately, though, with Peter giving her less of his time, she had begun to realize she shouldn't have neglected her own aspirations.

"Well, the good thing about cooking is that it's absolutely essential to life," Josh told her. "I practice every time I eat, which is three wonderful times a day. You, on the other hand, don't risk starvation if you don't practice a monologue."

No, not starvation, JoJo thought. "But I do feel like something's missing in my life," she said. "Acting was my whole world in high school and college. Now all I can count on is temping."

They both stared for a moment at the silent telephone.

"And I guess on some days I can't even count on that," JoJo joked, trying to sound more upbeat.

Josh clamped a hand on her shoulder and squeezed. A bolt of electricity shot out from the point of contact, so much so that JoJo tightened her grip around her coffee cup. It was supposed to be only an encouraging pat, but its effect was much stronger than that.

Josh gave her a smile of camaraderie, then let go. "Something's going to come together for you, JoJo. I saw you do that play reading when you and Peter first started going out. You're too talented to be on the shelf for long."

JoJo reached back into her memory. Instead of being buoyed by Josh's words, she experienced a fit of despair. "That was ages ago!"

Josh laughed. "Hey, you're all of what, twenty-three?"

"Twenty-three's *old*. When I was a kid I dreamed of being famous when I was nineteen, like Lauren Bacall." She chuckled and held out a lock of long curly black hair. "I guess all I had to do was look in the mirror to figure out that I was *nothing* like Lauren Bacall, huh?"

JoJo knew that Josh, an old movie buff like herself, would immediately recognize the comparison to Bacall, the statuesque blond star of forties films. But his next words surprised her. "Why are you always so hard on yourself? You know that actresses achieving that kind of success so soon is rare."

"I just wanted to be one of the lucky ones, I guess. Like Winona Ryder."

"She became famous as a teenager."

"Okay, so maybe it's too late for that."

"While you're at it, why don't you aspire to be Drew Barrymore? She was famous when she was six."

JoJo laughed. "All right, I understand it's too late for me to be a child prodigy."

"For most people it takes years of hard work to make a name for themselves," Josh said. "You just need to buckle down and start. And I know you will."

His words, though blunt, were encouraging. "You're right," she said. "I need to stop clinging to juvenile notions of what everything's going to be like."

"Don't get me wrong," Josh assured her. "I do that, too. But then I wake up and realize that I'm not going to graduate and jump right into a job as White House chef, or anything close."

They jabbered for nearly an hour over their eggs about school and work. For JoJo, it seemed that it had been years since she'd been able to talk to someone this freely about her dreams. She hadn't had many girlfriends since college, and though Peter was supportive, creativity wasn't his cup of tea. To him, a job was something you could work from nine to five, get promoted in and eventually retire from. He understood that JoJo wanted something different for herself, but he didn't have many helpful tips to help her along.

But Josh did, and talking to him was like a breath of fresh air. His mother had even been an actress in New York back in the seventies, so he knew as much as JoJo did about the world of theater and film.

When she looked up from her empty plate, it was going on eleven o'clock. "Guess I've got the day free, too," she said.

"Great. Let's hit the town."

Suddenly JoJo froze, remembering the weird attraction she'd felt to Josh the night before. And still felt. "I don't know...."

"C'mon," he cajoled. "I've got at least a hundred bucks until my MasterCard is maxed out. Let's live a little!"

"You mean go shopping?" After all their big talk about dedication and hard work, the idea sounded terribly frivolous.

"It's for my class," Josh said. "There's a book I want to get, and I love to look at the gadgets in expensive cooking stores. Don't you?"

JoJo laughed. ''No. Microwaving Lean Cuisine meals is about as creative as I get in a kitchen.''

''But you're sure to love the other part of the research I have planned.''

''What?''

''Lunch at this new Italian restaurant downtown. It's supposed to be great.''

''If it's great, I probably can't afford it,'' JoJo said morosely. The idea of staring into those baby blues for a few hours over a bottle of red was awfully tempting.

''My treat.'' When she hesitated, Josh added, ''You're even dressed for the downtown lunch crowd. There's no sense in having gotten all dolled up for nothing, is there?''

There was a little devil on her shoulder—one that looked suspiciously like Josh—telling her to say yes. She knew she wanted to. And he was right. What would it hurt, especially if he was paying?

But she couldn't. It just didn't feel right. She picked up her plate and marched to the sink to wash it, her mind made up. She turned to him to answer—and found herself staring into eyes the color of the Pacific Ocean.

Instead of giving him the firm refusal she had planned, she asked suddenly, ''When do we leave?''

''I can change in a second,'' Josh said, dashing back to his room.

JoJo scrubbed her plate and tried not to think about the light-headed feeling that had taken over her. It was only one day, she told herself. Tomorrow she would get back to business, back to worrying about her acting.

And more important still, back to Peter.

North Michigan Avenue was swarming with people, but Josh appeared to be in his element among the department-store shoppers and upscale boutiques. He was in a lively mood, even though they had walked and shopped, walked and shopped, until JoJo felt she was about to drop.

"You need a hat," he said as they stood in front of a window display of mannequins wearing every kind of hat imaginable.

Not for the first time, JoJo smiled wistfully and said, "I might want one, but I can't afford it." She'd always found window-shopping a bittersweet pastime for just this reason.

Josh looked at her as if he couldn't fathom having so much willpower. "By the time this day is through, we're going to find something in this whole great city you can afford, JoJo."

"Good luck," she said, laughing. They walked on, past a few more clothing boutiques and a small specialty toy store.

"Hold it right there!" Josh cried suddenly. He backed up and pointed enthusiastically to the toy store window. "Eureka!"

JoJo laughed and backtracked to see what had him so wound up. "This had better be good," she said.

"It's irresistible. And it's perfect for you, I promise."

She looked in the window and immediately burst out laughing. There, amid serious-looking wooden toys and very expensive imported dolls, was a five-foot inflatable plastic gorilla. "Thanks a lot!" she exclaimed.

"Hey, I bet you could afford it."

Unable to resist, they went inside and found out that the gorilla went for a mere eleven dollars. "You're right, Josh. A plastic gorilla is about the only thing I've seen today that I can afford. That's so depressing!"

"And eleven dollars is probably about ten dollars more than it's really worth." Josh shook his head as they left the store and stopped once more to ogle the bizarre item. "Who would buy such a cheesy thing?"

JoJo shrugged. "Someone desperate for novelty."

"Well, I don't know about novelty," Josh said, changing the subject, "but I am desperate for Italian food."

"Me, too," JoJo agreed.

Josh offered his arm for her to take, and they'd had so much fun just walking down the street that it seemed perfectly natural to link her arm with his. They were just friends goofing around, JoJo told herself as they strolled down the avenue together, then ducked down a side street. She hadn't had such spontaneous fun in a long time. Since college.

She remembered those early days with Peter and guiltily acknowledged that they had been fun, too. But that had been awhile back. These days, fun was the occasional Sunday afternoon at Wrigley Field in the summer or, as they had planned for tonight, watching a Bears game on the tube. And those activities were always planned weeks in advance. She couldn't remember the last time Peter had suggested doing something out of the blue.

Lunch, as promised, was delicious. JoJo had suspected that sitting across a table from Josh would be easy on the eye, which it was, but she also found his conversation engaging and funny. He was full of stories about his colorful mom the actress, and had a million tales to tell about his own exploits, too. Josh had a knack of being self-deprecating without coming off sounding like a jerk, and he must have inherited some of his mother's talents, because some of his impressions of people were dead-on.

Funny, she had known Josh for as long as she had known Peter, yet she and Josh had never been out alone before. Sitting across the table from him without having Peter next to her felt odd—as if they were going behind Peter's back. Yet Peter would be the last to object to his two best friends getting together.

So why did she feel a pang of guilt?

Josh ordered for them both, dishes he'd read about in restaurant reviews—wonderful crisp salads, focaccia bread, an antipasto plate to start, then chicken with parsley and pork piccata for the meal. After an hour of stuffing herself full of wonderful food, JoJo felt in danger of popping, and she was also a little tipsy from the bottle of merlot they'd been washing this prodigious meal down with.

"My family's Italian, and we never ate this well," she said as she sagged back into her chair.

Josh laughed. "My mother would occasionally get worked up into a gourmet-cooking frenzy. She would see herself as Julia Child one day, and the next we would be trying to swallow down rubbery omelettes. Being kids, we preferred Chef Boyardee to Julia Child any day."

"Of course. It doesn't take much to keep kids happy."

"I wish things were as simple now."

"Me, too!" JoJo took another comforting sip of wine, liking the loose, relaxed feeling it gave her. "When I was in school, I couldn't wait to get out and rent my own apartment and have a real life. I never dreamed that my apartment would be the size of a shoe box and that real life could be such a drag sometimes."

Josh's eyes twinkled—or maybe they were just glazed from all the wine. "I think I've found the perfect balance. Get the apartment, but stay in school. Never let your feet touch the ground."

"Never let your feet pound the pavement looking for a job, you mean?"

Josh winked. "Not as long as I can help it." He looked devilishly handsome, boyish and carefree.

JoJo shook her head in wonder—and in an attempt to clear it of its fuzziness. Josh considered mooching off his folks a full-time career. Nice work if you could get it, JoJo thought to herself. "I can't believe you and Peter live in the same apartment. He's such a workaholic."

"But that's why we get along so well," Josh told her. "Peter thinks I'm a slacker and I think he's Mr. Responsible, and we both respect each other's opinions. And since our goals are so completely different, there's no competition."

Just talking about Peter renewed JoJo's guilt about being out with Josh. "He's a great guy, isn't he?" She once more felt bad for not being nicer to him the night before.

"The best!" Josh agreed enthusiastically to cheer her mood. He held up his glass of wine. "Let's drink a toast to Peter, the working stiff who's nearest and dearest to our hearts!"

JoJo clinked her glass against his and drank up. The warm liquid soothed her somewhat. She would make it up to Peter. Thank heavens Josh appreciated him even when *she* was in danger of forgetting him.

"I have an idea," Josh said, interrupting her thoughts. "Peter's office is not too far from here. Let's walk over and drop in on him!"

For a moment, JoJo hesitated. "Peter's office is kind of stuffy," she said.

Josh slapped his palm on the table. "Which is precisely why we should go for a visit."

JoJo thought of poor Peter slaving away while they were having so much fun. Still . . . "He might not appreciate it."

Josh looked at her as if he couldn't believe what she was saying. "Peter?" he asked, dragging out his *r* a bit under the influence of the wine. "My bud? He needs us to cheer up his dreary little life!"

She giggled at the prospect of surprising Peter. "All right."

Josh signed for the bill. "Hear that noise?" He bent his ear closer to the table.

JoJo shook her head. "No, what noise?"

"My credit card just let out a groan," he said as he replaced the card in his wallet.

JoJo laughed. "I think you've had too much to drink."

"Me, too," he agreed as he split the remainder of the bottle between them. "Might as well finish it up for the road."

They tossed back one last glass of wine, left the restaurant and, laughing and skipping like kids, headed toward Peter's office to brighten up his day.

Three

Peter barely turned away from his computer terminal to pick up the phone ringing beside his desk.

"This is Peter," he answered, distracted by the columns of figures displayed on the screen in front of him.

There was a pause on the line, and then Glenda, the world's crankiest receptionist, giggled. "There's a delivery for you, Peter."

"For me?" This was weird. First of all, Glenda *never* giggled. And Peter rarely got stuff at the office—it wasn't even near his birthday or anything like that.

"Why else would I tell you that you had a delivery?" Glenda said tartly.

Now that sounded more like the normal Glenda. "Okay, I'll be right out." Still, he had an uneasy feeling as he hung up the phone.

His unease grew into something different as he went out to the reception area. Anticipation. Could his mother have sent him something? It was November, and she usually worried about his not dressing warmly enough. He hoped she hadn't sent him one of those big scarfs that she sometimes knit out of that multicolored yarn. He already had about twenty of them lying in a drawer in his apartment. They were just too embarrassing to wear to work.

But when he came through the door that led to the receptionist's desk by the elevator, there was no box in sight. Instead, Josh of all people was standing there, with a lopsided grin on his face.

"Surprise!" Josh yelled.

The word echoed in the stark windowless area. Lips pursed, Glenda shook her head.

Peter blinked. "Josh? What are you do—"

Suddenly JoJo's head poked out from behind Josh. "Surprise!" she said, her voice also sounding too loud for the plushly carpeted office.

"JoJo?"

At that moment, a five-foot plastic gorilla appeared on the other side of Josh. *"Surprise!"* Josh and JoJo yelled in goofy voices. Josh made the gorilla hop up and down in what was supposed to be excitement.

Peter forced a smile, though he couldn't work up much excitement himself over their plastic-gorilla humor. Glenda shot him a long-suffering look.

"Isn't he a howl?" JoJo said. "Josh and I brought him to keep you company."

Josh smirked as he registered Peter's speechlessness. "You don't have to thank us."

Peter's smile disappeared. They were drunk! He couldn't believe his girlfriend and his best friend would show up and make a scene in his office like this.

As if to magnify his embarrassment, his superior, Doug Feldman, chose that precise moment to come out to check his messages. Doug looked from the gorilla to JoJo to Peter and back at the gorilla again before pulling two pink slips off the message wheel. JoJo and Josh broke out giggling, causing Peter to squirm in discomfort.

"My cubicle barely fits a computer," he said nervously. "I don't have room for company."

Josh smiled. "Then I guess they'll just have to give you a bigger office."

"Guys…" Peter pleaded under his breath, knowing Doug was probably frowning on his unprofessional visitors.

"The gorilla's used to having his own space," JoJo explained.

Doug Feldman's lips turned up in a forced smile as he headed back toward the offices. They watched him go.

"Thanks a lot. That was my boss!" Peter told them in a low voice after Doug had rounded the corner.

"It was?" Josh's eyes widened innocently as he nudged the gorilla forward. "Then why didn't you introduce him to your new assistant?"

JoJo started laughing again and Peter rolled his eyes. How was he ever going to get them back on the elevators?

"Gee, guys, I really appreciate this, but I need to get back to work. Some of us *do* work, you know." He couldn't keep a trace of bitterness out of his voice.

Unfortunately, his Ward Cleaver tone sent them into renewed peals of laughter. They were like two kids who had been caught doing something naughty and now couldn't get over themselves.

"Bud, lighten up. It's not the end of the world."

"No, it's not," JoJo said, attempting to appear somber. "It's just an inflatable gorilla."

Their sober expressions lasted all of two seconds, and then they practically doubled over, howling with laughter. Tears spilled down JoJo's cheeks. "I can't believe you don't think this is funny, Peter," she admonished.

"I do," Peter said, trying to placate them.

But the lack of enthusiasm in his voice only tickled them more. Josh pulled a blank face. "This is Peter Lattimore, having fun at work," he said in a dead-serious monotone.

JoJo cracked up. It was a strain to be a good sport, but Peter forced a smile.

Josh wasn't finished yet, though. "This is Peter Lattimore, having fun with his gorilla at work." He put his arm around the inflated toy and kept his face a blank.

Even Glenda laughed at the goofy picture Josh made standing there with that ape. Great! Peter turned and, to his horror, he noticed that people had started to gather in the doorway. The UPS man came off the elevator with a delivery box and stared in amusement.

"Okay, okay," Peter said to his two crackpot friends, "you guys have had your fun." He prayed silently that the people in the doorway would go back to their offices. "Now, is there any reason you made the trip all the way over here?"

"Honestly, Peter," JoJo said, taking his hand, "we were just in the neighborhood and decided to drop by."

"And we picked up a friend for you along the way," Josh said, bringing the gorilla forward.

Peter let out a weary sigh when the UPS man hopped back on the elevator. "Gee, thanks," he said, looking humorlessly at the five-foot toy. He knew he should be a better sport about all this, but it wasn't very fun to realize that while he was slaving away at the boring office, his girlfriend and his roommate were off whooping it up.

Especially when they seemed intent on rubbing his face in their glee.

"Well," Peter said finally, "it's been great seeing you, but—"

"But you really do have to get back to work," JoJo finished for him. Her voice sounded petulant—as though he were somehow being unreasonable.

Peter pointed to his watch. "It's only two-thirty." Then he frowned. "Didn't you get assigned today?"

JoJo shook her head. "No, the agency didn't call me."

"So I decided to put her to work for me," Josh said. "She came with me to a new restaurant I'd been meaning to try."

They'd been together *all day?* "Must be nice to have such tough work to deal with," he said, looking from one to the other hesitantly, and maybe a little suspiciously.

"We enjoyed it," Josh said. "JoJo's a real trouper. I walked her all over the place."

Neither Josh nor JoJo looked guilty. Besides, if they were fooling around, why would they have come to visit him? Peter shook his head and admitted, "Wish I could have been there."

JoJo leaned over and kissed him on the cheek. "We should go there together sometime," she said.

Her face was flushed and happy, and suddenly Peter felt like a heel. Was he turning into a complete drip, or what?

He decided to chill out. "Well, I hope you guys have fun with the rest of the day." It was almost midafternoon. They'd probably head home now. "Don't forget the game tonight," he reminded JoJo.

Her eyes widened. "That's right, the game!" She turned to Josh and did some quick mental calculations. "We'll still have time, won't we?"

"Oh, sure," Josh said. He turned to Peter and explained. "We're going to the movies."

Peter's conciliatory smile froze.

JoJo squeezed his arm. "I thought I should take advantage of having a companion who likes something other than Jean-Claude Van Damme movies."

Peter felt completely left out, and disappointed that JoJo was going to the movies with Josh instead of with him. Not that he thought for a second there was any hanky-panky going on, but still . . . "In the middle of the afternoon?" he asked.

Josh smiled. "It's called a matinee, bud. We were going to run by the Music Box and see what foreign flicks were playing."

Peter hated foreign movies, but suddenly he would have given anything to be going with them. "Don't you have class tonight?" he reminded his roommate.

Josh looked at his watch, too. "That's right! Hey, Jo," he said, taking her arm as he leaned over to punch the down button for the elevator, "we'd better hit the road."

Like magic, the elevator doors opened and Josh and JoJo hopped inside. Suddenly Peter wanted to stop them, to talk to them some more, but it was too late.

"Bye, Peter," JoJo said, waving.

"Have a nice day," Josh added. He also waved as the elevator doors glided shut.

After they were gone, the silent lobby felt as if all the life had been sucked out of it. Peter let out a long breath and sent Glenda a "what could I do?" stare. He turned and slowly started heading back to his work area.

"Aren't you forgetting something?" Glenda asked him in her deadpan voice.

"Huh?" He turned back around and spotted the gorilla leaning up against the elevator. Great. He picked up the huge plastic toy and moped all the way back to his cubicle. Why was he stuck in this boring office all day while lucky Josh got to spend time with *his* girlfriend?

As he passed a conference room, someone made chimp noises. Clowns.

Life was just so unfair! Back in college he would have skipped class and taken JoJo to the movies himself. Well, maybe not—but at least the option would have still been there. Work wasn't something you could just drop. At least, he couldn't. Josh, who was being supported by his rich stepfather, could afford to have fun and be frivolous.

Back at his cubicle, Peter sank into his chair and pulled the clear plastic plug on the gorilla to deflate it. Naturally, it wasn't the kind from which the air rushed out fast, so he had to push on it really hard with his foot and listen to the wheezing sound it made as it lost air, which was probably driving the people around him nuts.

What really annoyed Peter was the fact that JoJo and Josh were both wrapped up in their creative work and never gave him credit for having landed a serious job making real money—which wasn't so easy for business majors just out of college in this day and age. He knew it was mercenary, but he wanted *things* in life, like a house, and a nice car and maybe kids someday. He wanted to get married sometime before he was eighty and try to have something approaching the American Dream. Was that so terrible?

That was why he was so obsessed with work these days. It was a drag, but until he was sure his job was secure and he was going to have enough money, he didn't know how he could make plans with JoJo, which to him meant marriage. He couldn't imagine settling down if it wasn't she he was sharing his life with. But they were both still pretty young, and JoJo wanted to pursue her acting career. He wondered if she ever thought of settling down the way he did.

Surely she didn't want to live in a grungy little efficiency for the rest of her life. That was the great thing about their being together—they complemented each other perfectly. At least he thought so. He was perfectly willing to carry the financial burden if they got married. Everything was a trade-off.

Suddenly Doug ducked his head around the opening to Peter's cubicle. He frowned at Peter, who was stepping on the plastic gorilla. "You haven't forgotten the meeting on the Simms-Berkeley account, have you?" he asked.

"I'll be right there," Peter said. He opened a cabinet drawer and pulled out the Simms-Berkeley file. His idle speculation about the future would have to wait.

That was the problem with working. He didn't even have time to dream anymore!

"You said you wanted to see this French movie, right?" Josh asked JoJo as they stood looking at the little board displaying the show times. They could see the French film, or an Irish film that was also supposed to be good.

"Is that okay with you?" she asked Josh.

"Mais oui," he said in his best French waiter voice. "I love anything that comes over that ocean!"

JoJo laughed and fished through her purse for admission money. "You're a nut."

"A nut for beautiful French women." He leaned close to her ear and whispered, "Or voluptuous Italian-Americans."

JoJo feared she was going to faint. The blood rushed to her head, and she strained to keep her voice light. "You're also a terrible flirt."

"Guilty," he agreed. They made their way in to take their seats.

The film was slow-moving but intense. Mimi and her husband, Jean, moved to Paris and rented an apartment next to an artist named Guy during the first five minutes of the film, and not much happened in the hour that followed. Not much, except about a million endless longing stares between Mimi and Guy in various stages of undress. Now Jean was going on a business trip, and Mimi and Guy were alone together. Mimi was naked in the tub, and Guy was next door, thinking about her.

And you didn't have to be Siskel or Ebert to figure out what was going to happen next....

They should have chosen the Irish movie, JoJo thought as Guy made his way down the hall. The Irish movie was a comedy.

She sat rigidly in her seat, leaning to the side away from Josh's elbow. She'd forgotten how tall Josh was. He sprawled all over the place in his tiny theater seat, and she was almost getting a cramp trying to avoid brushing her leg against his.

Of course she was being silly. What she felt for Josh was simple friendship—or, okay, maybe she had a little crush on him. It was nothing approaching the torrid passion that was happening on-screen. Not even close, she thought as the model-beautiful Mimi rose like Venus out of the tub. Only in French movies did women walk through the house with absolutely zip on.

JoJo scrunched down farther in her seat, dreading the next moments. It was as if a tight wire of tension connected her and Josh, and every time something sensual happened in the movie, an electric current traveled between them. Just like when he'd put his hand on her shoulder that morning, only now they weren't even touching....

Why had he made that crack about being attracted to Italian women? Was he really attracted to her, or was he only teasing? He had to know she was uncomfortable with whatever was developing between them.

Unfortunately, she feared she was uncomfortable because she was beginning to have feelings for Josh that for nearly two years had been reserved solely for another guy. Peter. Josh's best friend. And yet, she couldn't help the attraction she felt for Josh any more than Mimi could stop wanting Guy.

And there was Mimi, answering her door in nothing but a short, silky, transparent robe. Guy stared at her, stunned to find her practically undressed.

Josh cleared his throat softly, and in response, JoJo flattened herself against her armrest. Her whole body felt feverish and shaky, as if what was happening up there were actually happening to *her*. And in a way it was, she realized with sudden fear.

They had left poor Peter at worked and blithely run off together, well aware that something was building between them. If she had wanted to avoid Josh, she could have easily. But she'd been drawn to go out shopping with him, and to lunch and then to the movies. He'd seduced her without so much as kissing her.

Right now they weren't looking at each other, and yet she felt the same weak-kneed feeling that she would have had if they had been locked in an embrace as intimately as Mimi and Guy, who were now in the throes of passion.

Or maybe it was just the movie, she thought to herself. It had always been embarrassing to see steamy sex scenes with guy friends. In fact, she usually preferred to see spicy movies with Peter, or if he wouldn't watch them, by herself.

JoJo flinched as Guy and Mimi moaned in ecstasy. We *definitely* should have gone to the Irish movie, she thought.

Luckily, Jean came home in the next scene and the rest of the movie was about the bitter dissolution of Jean and Mimi's marriage. This part made JoJo sad, because poor Jean really didn't deserve what was happening to him. He was a nice guy.

Like Peter.

She thought guiltily of the way she and Josh had acted in Peter's stuffy office. What was the matter with her? Peter had obviously been embarrassed, and they had kept right on razzing him unmercifully in front of his co-workers—even his boss! It would be a miracle if Peter still wanted to speak to either of them after that episode.

She and Josh had behaved like school kids. In fact, her crush on Josh was juvenile, too; she felt like a teenager whose hormones had run amok. As the credits finally rolled, she wondered briefly whether there was some weird hormone thing that happened to women in their twenties. If there was, *Cosmopolitan* had failed to mention it.

"That was a fantastic movie, wasn't it?" Josh asked when the lights came up.

JoJo nodded enthusiastically. "Great." At least she hadn't been able to keep her eyes off the screen.

"That actress was really sexy," he said as they shuffled slowly out into the lobby behind the other audience members.

"Mmm." It always felt disconcerting to walk out of a matinee into the afternoon light. JoJo squinted and buttoned her coat as they approached the outside doors.

"I have an idea," Josh said.

JoJo frowned. Josh always seemed to be coming up with ideas—and they usually meant trouble.

"There's a coffee shop just down the street," he continued. "Let's go have a double espresso to wake me up before class. We can talk about the movie."

"Oh..." JoJo hesitated. "I don't know."

"C'mon," he told her. "What harm could it do?"

That was what she had thought about eating breakfast with Josh, and going to lunch with him and to the movies. Now she knew very well what harm it could do. It was one step toward busting up her solid relationship with Peter, and she wasn't sure she was ready to jeopardize that.

"I can't," she said determinedly. "I'm watching the football game with Peter tonight, and I really need to run by my apartment to check my mail."

Josh nodded. "Okay, some other time, then."

"Sure."

They chatted aimlessly on the way home. Josh must have sensed she was putting him off, because he didn't try to flirt with her anymore, even when he saw her to her doorstep.

JoJo ran up the three flights to her apartment, changed quickly into leggings and a floppy sweatshirt and collapsed onto her futon with a heavy sigh.

What kind of person was she, harboring secret feelings for her boyfriend's best friend? Peter and Josh grew up together, were best friends in high school and roommates through college. They probably knew more about each other than she knew about her own family. She was a slimeball for even thinking about coming between them.

She needed to cool down...maybe not see Josh for a while. Unfortunately, it was practically impossible to see

Peter without running into Josh, too. The two were like a boxed set. But she would just have to try to avoid Josh.

Poor Peter, she moaned to herself. He must hate her after this afternoon. What kind of girlfriend was she?

Josh threw things into his leather backpack without thinking. Most of the stuff he was including he probably didn't even need, but he wanted to make sure he didn't have to come back to the apartment while JoJo and Peter were watching their game. He didn't know why; he just felt funny about it.

He tried to focus on what he might do after class—maybe he would go hang out with friends, or park himself at a bar for a while. Poor Peter worked so much, he got the place to himself only on the rare times when Josh had an evening class, like tonight. The least Josh could do was give him some space to be alone with his girl.

Especially when he'd come within a hairbreadth of attempting to steal that girl just this afternoon....

As he was heading for the door, a key turned the lock on the other side. Josh dropped his hastily loaded backpack, sat quickly in his usual chair and started nonchalantly flipping through a *Sports Illustrated*. He didn't want it to look as if he were sneaking out.

"Hey, bud," he said when Peter walked through the door.

"Hey," Peter said. The guy looked beat. He set down his briefcase on the floor and shuffled over to the kitchen, opened the refrigerator and pulled out a soda. After taking a fortifying slug of caffeine and sugar, he asked, "Where's JoJo?"

Josh lifted his shoulders. "Home, I guess."

"I half expected her to be here when I came home."

Josh couldn't tell if Peter was disappointed or relieved that JoJo hadn't come back to the apartment with him. He looked at him, trying to gauge whether Peter had guessed that there had been a definite shift in the relationship between the three of them.

"Did you guys have fun at the movies?" Peter asked casually.

"Sure," Josh said. And he added lamely, "That JoJo, she's great." As if he had to tell Peter that!

Peter nodded. "What did you see?"

A vision ran through Josh's head of that French woman, Mimi, naked in the tub. And then later, in the bedroom with the artist fellow. Maybe it would be better if he didn't tell Peter too much about the plot. "Oh, some French thing."

"Was it any good?"

Josh barely remembered whether he liked it or not, just that there was this incredible feeling going on between him and JoJo the whole time. He'd felt sure she would want to go out afterward and at least talk, but then she'd insisted on cutting the afternoon short. Maybe that had been for the best, though. She was really cute, but this weird attraction he felt for her was making him feel edgy. It was as if he were a geeky teenager again, with a crush on somebody else's girlfriend.

Being a geeky twenty-four-year-old was definitely not acceptable, however. He would have to get over it.

"Earth to Josh...."

Josh was startled back to attention. "Huh?"

"The movie?" Peter reminded him.

"Oh, it was okay, I guess."

"Did JoJo like it?" he pressed.

"Yeah, I guess."

"You sure are talkative tonight, pal. About like you were when you jumped off my father's roof when we were eight."

That's about how he felt, too, Josh thought. Finding out he was attracted to Peter's girlfriend was almost like having the wind knocked out of him.

But on the other hand, what was the big deal? He was young, he was healthy, he liked women. That wasn't a federal offense. He hadn't even kissed JoJo. Not that he hadn't wanted to....

"Josh!"

Josh looked up, his eyes wide. "Huh?"

"You keep shorting out on me." He wagged a paternal finger at his roommate. "What's wrong, pal?"

Josh put the magazine aside and forced himself to look Peter in the eye. "Listen, Pete, I'm really sorry about this afternoon."

Peter shrugged. "It was no big deal."

"Yes, it was. I was acting like a real jerk." He quirked an eyebrow up. "Guess I shouldn't have had that bottle of wine for lunch."

Peter waved a hand in dismissal. "Actually, I laughed about it to myself all afternoon as I tried to deflate that stupid gorilla."

Josh shook his head, still amazed by the toy. "Why on earth do they make stuff like that?"

Peter looked at him with a grin. "Because they know there are a lot of people out there with arrested development who will buy it."

"Very funny," Josh said. "It was JoJo's fault, anyway."

His friend perked right up after hearing JoJo's name. "It was?"

Josh nodded. "She wanted to get you a present and that was all she could afford that we saw."

Peter let out a sigh. "Well, I would have thought it was funny, too, if I hadn't been having such a lousy day."

Josh grimaced. "Guess our appearance didn't help much. Did it get better?"

"Yeah, my boss said I did a really good job on this account I've been working on." He said the words almost as if he didn't believe them. "I think I might actually get another promotion before Christmas."

"That's great!" Josh exclaimed. "We'll have to go out and celebrate."

"We should at least wait till it happens," Peter said prudently.

"Heck, why not celebrate before, during and after?" Suddenly, Josh's face turned from festive to fearful as he glanced at the apartment around them. "I hope you don't become too rich, though. You'll want to move out of this dump into someplace I can't afford."

Peter laughed. "I wouldn't worry about it. By the time that happens, you'll be living in Paris or somewhere."

"That reminds me!" Josh jumped up. "I'm going to be late!" He sped toward the door and turned back once before he left. "Enjoy the game tonight, bud."

"Okay, pal."

Peter watched Josh go with something like relief. He'd been afraid that Josh was going to be angry at him for behaving like such a pill this afternoon. They'd been friends forever, and he didn't want disagreement over a stupid prank to end their friendship.

Now he had to make sure it didn't ruin his relationship with his girlfriend, either. He picked up the phone and dialed JoJo's number.

She answered after one ring. "Hello?" Her voice sounded breathless.

"Jo, it's me," Peter said. "Were you waiting for the phone to ring?"

"No. I was just... thinking." Her voice sounded distracted.

"I talked to Josh," he said.

"Oh, really?"

Peter laughed at her sudden curiosity. "Yeah, I usually do, you know. He lives here."

"I guess talking to him would be a hard thing to avoid," she agreed.

They both chuckled lamely, then there was a short pause. "Josh said you went to a French movie. How did you like it?"

"I didn't."

"Josh said you did."

JoJo hesitated a moment, then blurted out, "I lied. He seemed to like it, so I said I did, too."

"Peer pressure?" Peter asked. He was beginning to get a little nervous. Everyone was acting so strange! Especially when it came to that movie. . . .

"I guess," JoJo said.

Peter took a deep breath and attempted to strike a light-hearted tone. "So, are you coming over to watch the game? It starts pretty soon."

There was a long pause. "I can't, Peter."

Peter took this in and tried not to sound disappointed. "Oh, okay."

JoJo jumped in to explain. "I'm sorry, Peter. I know this sounds stupid, but I think I might have drunk too much at lunch or something. I don't feel too good."

"Josh said something similar."

"Josh is sick?" JoJo asked, her voice worried. "Didn't he go to class?"

"Yes, he went." Peter laughed. "You both sure are moody tonight. Now you know why I don't like foreign movies."

"I think I just need to sleep," JoJo explained.

"Okay, I'll let you get your rest. But before I go, I wanted to apologize."

"*You* want to apologize? What for?"

"For being such a killjoy this afternoon. I don't know what got into me. You must wonder sometimes whether I'm turning into a complete drip."

"You?" JoJo sounded astonished. Peter could imagine her sitting forward and waving her hands as she spoke into the receiver. *"I'm* the one who needs to apologize."

"You guys were just having fun."

"We were behaving like we were twelve!" she corrected in her firmest voice. "All afternoon I've been so ashamed."

"Is that why you're acting so strange?" Peter felt relieved. "I know I acted like a sourpuss while you guys were there, but I understood, I really did."

"I still feel bad," JoJo said.

"Well, don't," Peter insisted. He couldn't wait to have the whole gorilla incident finally behind them. "Now how 'bout those Bears? Are you sure you don't want to come over?"

"Oh . . . I don't think so. Do you mind?"

"I'd rather see it with you than without you," he said sincerely, "but if you don't feel well, I understand. Do you need anything?" Her fridge was always empty, partly because she always brought stuff over to his apartment.

"No, I'm okay."

"Are you sure? I could get some take-out and bring it over."

"That's sweet, but I'll be fine."

"Let me know if you change your mind," Peter told her.

"You know what? I think you must be the nicest guy in the world."

"Uh-oh. Aren't nice guys supposed to finish last?"

"Only in sports, Peter." He could imagine her gorgeous face breaking into a smile. "Romance is different."

Every time he talked to her, it seemed he fell a little deeper in love with her. "Sleep tight, JoJo," he said.

"See you soon," she said.

He hung up the phone slowly, lost in a jumble of emotions—desire, disappointment and anticipation for the next time he would see her. Maybe if he took a walk, he thought, it would help him sort things out.

He decided to go to Razzles and watch the game on the big-screen television they had there. Nursing a beer wouldn't be as fun as cuddling with Jo, but he needed his football, especially after the stressful day this had turned out to be.

Four

Peter's family lived in Newland, Wisconsin, and usually JoJo loved to visit. Her own experience of Smalltown, USA, was practically nil. She had grown up in New York City, until her parents divorced and her mother, a native Chicagoan, moved JoJo and her brother back to Illinois to be near her family. JoJo still missed New York sometimes, but she didn't like to visit her father, who usually had a parade of women going through the apartment, and whose idea of quality time was giving her a twenty and cab fare to go to the Metropolitan Museum of Art.

The Lattimores couldn't be more different from the Giamattis if they tried. Peter's mom was a housewife, and his father ran an insurance company. They lived in a picture-perfect wood frame house with a big yard, picket fence, the whole bit. Several times a year, Peter and his two older sisters and older brother would descend on the house to visit, Grandma Lattimore would come over and the place would be so full of family that it would feel on the verge of bursting. Even so, they always welcomed JoJo with open arms.

Thanksgiving was a must-attend affair for the Lattimores. JoJo had gone the year before and enjoyed herself, but she hadn't been looking forward to this trip quite as much. Things just weren't going very well between her and Peter, and she wasn't sure how she would take all the ribbing they usually received. His family was forever teasing them about settling down and getting married. The times before she hadn't minded this very much, but back then she and Peter were more solid with each other.

It wasn't that they weren't getting along. On the surface, things were back to normal between them, with a few differences. After that day at the movies, JoJo had avoided Josh for a while, preferring to meet Peter after work and go back to her apartment for a change. She made a concerted effort to do things Peter liked to do, and to avoid dwelling too much on the differences between them.

The trouble was, she was always aware that she was making an effort. Even when Peter wasn't doing anything wrong, she felt herself getting moody, restless and bored. What was the matter with her? It was almost as if she were just tired of Peter—but how could you get tired of someone who was nearly perfect?

She was constantly making up excuses for her moodiness—some days she decided Peter took her for granted, others she decided he was bored with her. But deep inside, she knew that their problems were stemming from *her,* and her feelings, more than from anything Peter was doing.

"I really hope Ellen doesn't make that squash casserole again," Peter said.

He was driving and JoJo was sitting in the passenger seat. The weather was amazingly clear and mild, so they were barreling down the highway with the rest of the holiday travelers.

Last year, the weather had been slushy and traffic had been a nightmare. All the way back from Newland, they had been laughing about Ellen's squash-and-mayonnaise casserole, which had been just dreadful but which no one in Peter's family had had the nerve to criticize. As the oldest girl, Ellen somehow thought she was naturally the best cook— even though all the evidence refuted this misconception.

Josh, whose mother lived right next door to the Lattimores, had gotten a big kick out of this, natch. He'd rescued them by running next door and bringing back all the Tums he could root out of the medicine cabinet.

Remembering their wisecracking trip home, JoJo grew almost nostalgic. Then she shook her head to clear it. Nostalgia over heartburn? That was pretty stupid!

"I hope not, too," JoJo agreed. "Although at least this year we'll know better than to take heaping helpings of it if she does bring it."

There was a long pause before Peter asked, "It's not the same without Josh along, is it?" He was obviously remembering the same things she had been.

"No, it's not." Still, she was glad. Peter's Volkswagen would have seemed claustrophobic with the three of them this time. Josh had decided at the last minute that he would go back to Iowa to visit some friends from college who had asked him to come out.

JoJo wondered whether Josh was still feeling the same tension she was and he had used the trip as an excuse to avoid being around her. "Did Josh ever get back in touch with Sandy?" she asked, trying to sound as if she were just making idle conversation.

Peter laughed. "No, I think he was glad to get rid of her. Don't you remember?"

She turned her face away, sure it had turned a telltale shade of red. Did she remember! She would never forget watching Josh on the phone and thinking for the first time how attracted she was to him. "He's awfully cavalier in the way he treats women, isn't he?"

"Josh?" Peter said, astounded that she even asked. "He's a bounder."

"I'm sure he's not that bad," JoJo argued, though she wasn't sure why.

One light brown eyebrow shot above the rims of Peter's glasses. "*Please,* I've lived with the guy. He's my best friend in the whole world, but if I were a woman, I'd avoid him like the plague." He looked at her, then reached his hand over and took her hand in his. "Unless he's just a friend, of course, like he is to you. There isn't a better friend in the world than Josh."

JoJo smiled, then looked out the window again. She wondered if Peter would feel that way if he could have seen the way Josh had looked at her after that movie. . . .

"Peter, have another helping of Ellen's squash."

The room became quiet and Peter's smile froze in place as all eyes turned on him. "Sure," he said weakly.

The man should get a humanitarian medal, JoJo thought. After last year, no one was touching that casserole—except Peter, of course, who would have died before hurting Ellen's feelings. He'd already choked down two helpings of the stuff, and now he put another dollop on his plate.

"I'm awfully full, though," he warned. "I don't know if I can finish it all."

Ellen beamed. "I'm so happy you like it, Peter. I'll have to wrap up the leftovers for you and JoJo to take home."

Peter and JoJo nodded and smiled. With the entire family's attention focused on them, JoJo had a terrible premonition of what was coming next. Her stomach clenched with dread.

Naturally, it was outspoken Grandma Lattimore who brought the subject up. "When are those two finally going to tie the durn knot?" she exclaimed. Grandma Lattimore had a knack for talking about you as though you'd just left the room.

The rest of the family members—married people all—eagerly took up this topic.

"Speak up. When's the wedding day, you two?" Peter's other sister, Tracy, asked.

Even though she'd seen the subject coming a mile away, JoJo couldn't help blushing. It wasn't that she was embarrassed just about having the eyes of the entire table zooming in on them, though that was uncomfortable enough. She also felt bad about her and Peter having problems—as though her fleeting attraction to Josh meant that she didn't deserve to be eating at the Lattimores' holiday table. Especially not when they practically had the two of them married off already.

"Yeah, Peter, when are you going to get up the nerve to pop the question?" his brother, Ben, prodded.

She and Peter exchanged awkward stares.

"If you don't hurry, some other fellow is going to snap her right up," his mother said.

JoJo, thinking guiltily of Josh, blurted out, "No, they won't!" Everyone stared at her, including Peter, puzzled by her hasty reaction, and she mentally groped for a way to explain. "I mean..."

"She only has eyes for Peter," Peter's mom finished for her with an exaggerated sigh. "Isn't that romantic?"

"Ah, young love." Tracy, who was all of twenty-six, took the hand of her husband, Tom. "When you stop looking at other men, you know you've found the one."

JoJo felt herself pale. Did that mean Peter wasn't the one for her? Could his family tell that her eye had been straying? And worse, could Peter?

"That's right," Ellen drawled. She had been divorced once and was the cynic of the family when it came to romance. "Once your eye stops straying, it's a sure sign you're going to get sucked into a lifelong commitment."

Ben took the practical approach and spoke to JoJo and Peter directly. "I don't see what the big deal is. You like each other, it's been two years. Rents being what they are in Chicago, seems to me that you'd want to move in together, save some money."

His wife, Marcy, who was eight months pregnant, nodded in agreement. "It's cheaper, that's for sure."

"Only if they're married, Ben," Peter's mother admonished.

"That's right!" Grandma Lattimore shook her head and clucked her tongue at the gall of the younger generation. "In my day, people just didn't run around—what's the expression you all use?—*shacking up.*"

"That's right," Peter's father stalwartly agreed. "Marriage is a commitment, an obligation."

"Thanks, everyone," Peter said. "You make marriage sound so appealing, JoJo will probably flee in panic when I do ask her."

JoJo turned to him, her mouth wide in astonishment. He made it sound as if he were actually thinking about asking her! Was he? What would she say if he did?

"Oh, no!" the family cried in unison, their eyes blinked open wide, as if they were afraid they'd actually scared JoJo.

"Marriage is truly wonderful," Tracy assured her. "If you have doubts, come talk to me, not Ellen."

"That's not fair," that sister defended. "I have plenty of good things to say about marriage. Just not always about husbands."

"Ellen!" several people cried at once.

"Nice to know I'm appreciated," Jerry, Ellen's second husband, said.

Ellen patted him placatingly on his balding head and turned to JoJo. "Don't worry. Not everyone's as cynical as I am. And Peter's the nicest of all the family."

"That's right," everyone agreed.

His father nodded. "Best looking, too, in my opinion."

JoJo could swear poor Peter was blushing. He hated these terrible discussions about marriage with his family as much as she did.

Luckily, his mother rescued him. "How about dessert and coffee?" she asked. Everyone groaned, but after a little coaxing they admitted that they would have just a sliver—it was a family tradition. But to the Lattimores, a "sliver" usually meant a huge hunk that you could never finish in a million years.

JoJo laughed sometimes at the predictability of the Lattimores. To her, the blond clan seemed to have stepped right out of a Norman Rockwell painting. JoJo couldn't remember the last time her own family had sat down to a real Thanksgiving dinner, with turkey, dressing and the whole nine yards. The last big dinner she'd had at her mother and stepfather's was before her brother, Steve, had gone off to Germany with the army. They'd ordered pizzas.

Even the Lattimores' quirks seemed to be set in stone. Ellen was the cynic and Tracy the chipper one. Mrs. Lattimore doted on the boys shamelessly, which sometimes got on the sisters' nerves. Grandma Lattimore could always be counted on to break a silence. Yet, even though they had their problems, no one ever started yelling or questioning the way things were done.

Sometimes she wondered how she would fit in with these people if Peter did ever ask her to get married. . . .

She picked up her empty dinner plate and carried it to the kitchen, which had already become a pie-and-coffee-serving assembly line, with Tracy, Ellen and Mrs. Lattimore dishing everything up efficiently. Meanwhile, the men came in with empty serving bowls and silverware. The Lattimores were such a perfect family, they even had the men trained to clear the table!

All that industriousness made for a traffic jam in the kitchen, though. And in the midst of all the madness, there was a knock at the door.

"I'll get it," JoJo volunteered, glad to have something useful to do. She sidestepped around several people and cracked the kitchen door. Outside stood a woman JoJo recognized as Josh's mother, whom she had met but never really spoken to.

Barb Delaney looked as glamorous as if she'd stepped off New York City's Fifth Avenue instead of a side yard in Wisconsin. She was tall and thin, with high cheekbones and a long swanlike neck, like Audrey Hepburn. Her coloring was just like that of Josh, her son by her first marriage, and she wore her clothes with the same panache that he did, too. Underneath her red cashmere coat and long silk scarf decorated with huge white lilies, she had on a simple, elegant black dress that hugged her lithe figure. She wore a pair of pumps with four-inch heels as casually as if they'd been sneakers.

"You're Josh's mother, aren't you?" JoJo asked.

The woman beamed at her, showing perfectly straight white teeth. "Please, darling, I'm *Barb*. And you're JoJo— Joshua told me you would be here."

"He did?" JoJo was sure she was slack-jawed with astonishment. Josh had spoken about her to his *mother?* Her heart started pumping like an engine. What had he said?

Barb nodded, handed JoJo the covered pie plate in her hand and swept on inside. "He said we'd have the most fabulous time talking together. I want to hear all about how your acting is going."

In the next minutes, Barb was busy greeting all the Lattimores and their in-laws and their children, but once the group finally sat down to have dessert, she secured a place next to JoJo.

"Have you been going on auditions?" she asked as soon as it was boisterous enough in the room to have a private conversation.

JoJo shook her head, embarrassed. "I know I should, but..."

"But you've lost confidence since college."

JoJo opened her eyes in surprise. It was as if Barb could read her mind! "Yes. I knew things would be difficult, but I never dreamed—"

"How competitive the theater truly is?" Barb asked, lighting a long menthol cigarette. JoJo thought smoking was a pretty stupid habit, but Barb made it look as sophisticated as it had in old black-and-white movies.

"Joshua said you had a wonderful singing voice."

He did? "I did a few musicals in college. You know, like *West Side Story.* But that was Iowa. I think they saw my long black hair and decided I would be a great Puerto Rican."

Barb laughed her raw throaty laugh, and JoJo was completely captivated by her. She couldn't believe she'd never talked to Josh's neat mother before. "You're being too modest. Joshua told me you were a wonderful actress."

Peter, who had been eavesdropping on the other side of JoJo, leaned in to join them. "Don't let her fool you," he told Barb. "She is wonderful."

Barb placed a long-nailed hand decorated with big chunky rings on his shoulder and said, "You *must* encourage Jo to go on more auditions. You *must.* An actress needs encouragement. Constant encouragement!"

"I told JoJo just the other day that she looked just like this woman on the Italian spaghetti sauce commercial," Peter joked.

Barb's full red lips pursed into a scolding frown. "Peter, my boy, that's *not* encouragement. I've seen the commercial—that woman can't even read cue cards properly." She let out another full-throated laugh.

It was rare these days that JoJo got to talk to a person who had actually made a living in the theater, and she wanted to take advantage of the opportunity. "Josh said you worked in soap operas back in New York," she prompted.

For the next hour, Barb regaled her with stories of working on daytime television—which was nowhere near as glamorous as one would suspect. She had plenty of tales concerning bullying directors, lines that had to be memorized in ten minutes and nights spent taping and retaping the same scene until the small hours of the morning. Barb had even had a supporting role as a vixen on one show for a whole season before she met Josh's father.

JoJo was completely enthralled, especially when Barb offered to give her advice on what monologues she should use on auditions, and whether her head shots—eight-by-ten photos actors gave to casting agents and directors—were appropriate.

"That would be great!" JoJo exclaimed gratefully. "I got mine taken in college, and I'm afraid they don't look professional enough for Chicago."

"I like those pictures of you," Peter interjected. He'd been listening off and on to their discussion. "I've got one of them at my office."

"A good professional photo is essential if you want to make an impression," Barb advised, dismissing Peter's biased opinion. "Absolutely *essential.*"

JoJo frowned. "I wish I had one here I could show you."

"Oh, darling, I come into town to visit Joshua all the time," she said, bestowing a hand on JoJo's shoulder. "I would love to take you out for lunch with us."

JoJo's face lit up like a neon sign. "That would be terrific!"

"In fact, I often like to tag a matinee while I'm in town. We should pick up tickets and make a day of it. Or maybe go to a museum."

"I would love to," JoJo said. Then she noticed Peter frowning at her. "Of course, I'd have to know in advance, because I temp...."

"Then that's perfect!" exclaimed Barb enthusiastically. "I'll tell you the next time I'm coming into town, and you can arrange to be off that day. What a smart girl you are to keep your schedule flexible!"

JoJo flushed, feeling for one illogical moment as if she were the only aspiring actress in Chicago who had figured out the advantages of temping. "I hope you come soon," she said, unable to keep her eagerness in check. "I'm really looking forward to it."

Barb winked. "Me, too, darling. We'll have a grand time together, you and Joshua and I."

Barb and JoJo continued jabbering away, alternately talking shop and making plans for what they could do when they met in Chicago. Only Peter seemed to realize that he hadn't been factored into their cozy little equation.

Five

"**S**he is *soooo* cool!" JoJo exclaimed for the hundredth time since they'd gotten back into the car. "I can't imagine what it would be like to have such a neat person for a mom, can you?"

Peter's face remained a blank.

"I mean, don't you think she's the greatest?" JoJo asked. She was flushed and excited, as if she'd just met a movie star. "No wonder Josh is such a neat guy, having grown up around her. Don't you think she looks just like Anjelica Huston?"

"You didn't seem so interested in her last Thanksgiving," he pointed out.

"I'd never really talked to her before. She's so sophisticated. I can't believe she lives in Wisconsin." She said the name of his home state as though it were as remote and culturally barren as a desert island.

Peter gripped the steering wheel a little harder. They'd been driving for a half hour, and JoJo had talked about nothing besides Barb, and what a great person Barb was, and how much she wanted to be like Barb.

He knew it was petty, but JoJo had never talked that way about *his* mother before, or mentioned how interesting *his* family was or called *him* a neat guy. Maybe his family wasn't exotic enough, or eccentric, though wasn't that in the Lattimores' favor? JoJo was always complaining about her own family, especially her overaged playboy father. Peter would have thought he was all the eccentric family she needed.

Apparently not. He couldn't forget the horrified look on JoJo's face when his family had started razzing them about getting married. She'd looked terrified, as if she were afraid he would pop the question then and there. Suddenly he wondered what her answer would have been if he had.

"I wish I were that tall," JoJo said, heedless of his silence, "instead of being so squat and chunky."

"You're not chunky," Peter said.

"Oh, please! Barb said the camera puts ten pounds on a person. Can you imagine what that would do to my thighs?"

"I doubt they do many close-ups on women's thighs, Jo."

She sent him a "you've-got-to-be-kidding" look. "You obviously didn't see *Basic Instinct*." She sighed. "I bet Barb could have played that role."

"Barb? You've never even seen her act," Peter said disbelievingly. "I grew up next door to this woman, if you'll recall. She might have been an okay actress once, but I just remember her as my best friend's mom who burned cookies and dressed funny."

"You were just a stupid kid," JoJo said dismissively, then gushed, "How about her voice! It's so sexy and husky, like Kathleen Turner's voice."

"That's because she smokes, Jo," Peter said, a little exasperation coming through now. "Her voice sounds like that because her poor throat has been ravaged from years of inhaling tar. You think that's cool?"

JoJo rolled her eyes impatiently. "You sound like the Surgeon General or something. I just said she had a cool voice."

"You've said the word *cool* about three million times in thirty minutes," Peter pointed out.

"I think you're exaggerating," JoJo answered, and before Peter could open his mouth to speak, she yelled excitedly, "Oh! And did you hear what she said about giving me the name of one of her old friends who teaches acting classes in Chicago? Wasn't that really nice of her to think to do?''

"Yeah."

For the first time since they'd gotten in the car, she looked at Peter really closely. "You don't sound very excited."

"Jo..." Peter sighed, then admitted, "Yes, it was a nice thing for her to say. Whether she follows up on it remains to be seen."

"You sound as if you don't expect her to."

"Well, what does it matter if she does?" Peter asked. "Are you really going to commit to taking classes?"

"Why not?"

He shrugged. "You've lived in Chicago for over two years and you've never talked about doing that before."

"That doesn't mean it's not a good idea. Barb said that all actors should take them, to hone their craft."

Peter groaned. "Can we please talk about something besides Barb, and what Barb said?"

"I can't believe you!" JoJo said hotly. "You seem to resent the fact that Barb gave me a little encouragement."

"Like *I* don't give you encouragement?"

"Sure. But you're not an actress, with real experience, who can give me practical advice," JoJo argued.

"Oh, I'm sorry. I'm only a humble accountant." He shuddered dramatically. "I could never truly empathize with you *creative* types."

JoJo's eyes narrowed into slits. "I'm beginning to wonder whether you care about my career at all."

"What career?"

JoJo's mouth parted in surprise and blood rushed to her face in response to her shock and anger. "Pardon me?"

"I said, what career? You're a temp!"

Peter had never gotten this upset with her before—he rarely lost his temper at all—but now that he'd started, he found it difficult to cool down. "As far as I can tell, *I'm* the only one doing any real work around here," he raved. "And then I get needled because I'm not a good sport when everyone else is playing hooky."

JoJo huffed out a breath. "Are you still upset about that day?"

"It's not just that," Peter said. "It's always being regaled with big tales of what everyone else is *planning* to do. Josh is going to be a famous chef, you're going to win an Oscar. At least Josh goes to chef school. You haven't even been on an audition in months! When does reality set in for you people?"

His words held some truth, but that didn't make them any easier for JoJo to digest. "I think you're jealous," she said with indignation, so mad, she was practically quaking. "No one forced you to become a working stiff, Peter."

He resented the insult. "I do what I do because that's what I'm good at. I just get mad because I want to see you succeed, too, and you don't even seem to be taking baby steps toward getting what you want. And meanwhile you put everything else in your life on hold."

Especially me, he wanted to add, but he didn't have the nerve.

"If you're so worried about my career, I don't see why you're so hot and bothered when someone offers to help me," JoJo retorted hotly.

"I just don't want you staking your hopes on the whims of some flighty woman. I thought it was strange that she picked you out to talk to like that."

JoJo sputtered in indignation, "Why does it strike you as strange that someone might want to talk to me?"

"I didn't mean it that way—"

She cut him off. "Don't worry, Peter. I'm not staking my hopes on what Barb can do for me, or anyone else. Starting now, I'm turning over a new leaf." She crossed her arms and made a point of turning away from him to look out the window.

Her words sounded ominous to him, as though she were ready to call it quits on their relationship. Was she? Peter didn't press the matter—it was obvious that neither of them was in the mood to give an inch.

They drove the rest of the way into Chicago in tense silence. Peter couldn't say now why he had become so angry, but he wished he hadn't. Arguing never solved anything.

And yet, he couldn't bring himself to apologize, either. Why should he, when he was right?

Peter slowed down as he pulled onto JoJo's street. His mind struggled to find words that would put things right between them again, but the search was fruitless. Before he could think of anything, he was pulling up in front of her door.

"You can just let me out," JoJo said brusquely.

"Jo…"

"What?" she asked, her voice terse. Her dark eyes were narrowed defensively, and her face showed the strain that he also felt inside.

"I'll call you later, okay?" he asked.

"Whatever," she said, then added automatically, "and thanks for taking me home for the holiday. And thank your mom again if you talk to her."

He nodded.

JoJo got out and reached into the back seat for her weekend bag. "I'll talk to you soon," she said, and a minute later she disappeared inside her apartment building.

Follow her, a voice inside his head instructed. *Don't let her go.*

But another equally forceful voice advised that they both needed space. He took a last glance up at her window, saw her lights pop on and then drove the rest of the way home.

* * *

"Werner, Schell and Fitzhugh," JoJo chirped into the receiver with a perkiness she didn't feel. After a day of saying the name of the law firm where she was working as a receptionist, it came as easily to her as breathing. "May I help you?"

She transferred the caller, sank down against her leather swivel chair and stared at the newspaper ads in front of her. There were several open-call auditions for women—but did she have a chance? She sighed and circled several of the ads with a blue highlighting marker.

As angry as he'd made her on Sunday, she knew Peter was right. All these months, she'd been dreaming, not working toward her goal. But he didn't understand how important it was to have a contact who really knew the business. Meeting Josh's mother had gotten her revved up to try to go out and audition again almost as much as Peter's stinging comments had.

Always true to his word, he'd called her Sunday evening. He and Josh, who had just returned from Iowa, were sitting around watching "Sixty Minutes," as usual, and he'd asked her if she wanted to drop by. He tried to make it sound as if nothing had happened, but JoJo knew that going over there would have been horrible. She was still mad at Peter for chewing her out, and the last person she needed to see was Josh.

That had been three days ago; Peter hadn't called again. She worried now that he wasn't going to.

That thought was completely depressing. Peter was the best friend she had in Chicago. For nearly two years, they had done everything together, been everything to each other. Maybe it had been too much, or they were too young. But that seemed impossible. Her own mother had been only nineteen when she got *married*.

And look what happened to that union, she thought despairingly. Her father had walked out on her mother for a reason no more substantial—or specific—than wanting his freedom. What he meant, JoJo supposed, was freedom from a wife and kids, so he could run around with a million women.

One thing was sure, life in Chicago could be tough, and it would be twice as hard trying to get by without Peter. She thought of how nice he had been in the past, bringing her food when she was too sick to get out of bed to make it herself, cheering her up with Cubs tickets on boring summer weekends, remembering her birthday when everyone else besides her mother forgot it.

She looked down at the blue circles she had made on the newsprint. Without Peter's support, going out on auditions would be pretty rough, too. But she couldn't let herself become completely dependent on him, she reminded herself. She owed it to herself to persevere whether he was with her or not.

A line buzzed again and she picked up the receiver and transferred the call. Then, without putting the phone back down, she punched in the number given in one of the ads.

The phone picked up after two rings. "Yeah?" asked a voice.

JoJo felt her hand shaking and forced it to stop. "Hi, I'm calling about the audition listed in the paper."

"Yeah?"

What a great phone manner this guy had, JoJo thought. For some reason, knowing that she was at least a better receptionist than the person on the other end of the line gave her courage. "I wanted to audition, so I need to know when the call takes place."

"Tonight."

There was a pause as JoJo panicked. "Tonight? As in, this evening?"

"Seven o'clock sharp. Bob, the director, doesn't like it when people are late, either. Just a word of warning."

"Thanks," JoJo said, "I'll be there."

She was about to hang up when the guy on the other end called out, "Hey, lady!"

"Yes?"

"Don't you want the address?"

JoJo took it down, shaking her head the whole time. Stage fright was already setting in.

From her apartment, it wouldn't take her long to get to the address the man had given her. That allowed her just about an hour to prepare a monologue, which was impossible, but it would have to suffice. And she had to figure out what to wear, and dust off those head shots.

She counted down the minutes until the end of the day. At five-fifteen she was on the elevator, and she hit the street at a walk so brisk, it was almost a trot. When she reached her apartment, she took the flights up at a run. Her bookshelf was crowded with scripts, and she quickly picked out one of the monologues she'd done often in college and began reading it over and over. She chose a stretchy fitted red dress from her closet, and as she dressed, she recited the monologue and found to her surprise that it was coming back to her easily.

Her legs felt rubbery by the time she locked her apartment, and the butterflies were beginning to gather in her stomach. Why did people do this to themselves? she wondered. Somehow the familiar question, which she used to ask herself a million times in college, made her feel her old self again.

She was prepared to dash down the building's steps, but when she opened the outside door that led to the stoop, she found Peter waiting for her. He was carrying a shopping bag. For a moment, he seemed as surprised to see her as she was to see him.

"Peter!" she cried. "What are you doing here?"

"I was just coming up for a visit." He held up the bag. "Josh made a feast at school today, so I brought over a dinner for two."

JoJo looked at the shopping bag and felt her stomach grumble. She'd completely forgotten to eat, which probably wasn't smart. Nevertheless, she had only thirty minutes to make it to the audition—and the cranky phone person had even told her not to be late.

"I'm sorry, but I've got to run, Peter. I've got an appointment."

Slowly Peter's eyes noticed the eye-catching outfit she was wearing. "You look terrific," he said, pushing his glasses up on his nose nervously. His eyes were wary as he obviously tried to discern whether she was going out on a date.

She debated putting him at ease, because in a sense it would be admitting that he had been right in their argument on Sunday. In the end, though, his sad brown-eyed gaze made up her mind. "Actually, I'm going on an audition."

He released a breath in relief; then his eyes widened with surprise. "You sure move fast once you've made up your mind!"

"And I've really got to move fast if I'm going to make it there. Maybe dinner some other time?"

He nodded vigorously. "Do you want me to come with you?"

She smirked. "And hold my hand?" She couldn't help thinking that Peter was awfully enthusiastic once she was doing what he wanted her to do.

Of course, it was what *she* wanted, too.

"I could be your agent," he offered.

"Thanks, but no thanks."

"It was just a thought." He shrugged, then leaned forward and pressed a kiss against her cheek. "In any case, break a leg."

A little swell of warmth built inside her at the gesture. Peter really was a prince. He was almost too nice. So why couldn't she shed her residual anger from their one fight in two years?

"I'll talk to you later." JoJo smiled, then turned and hurried toward the El, her heart brimming with optimism. She felt lucky to have a friend like Peter—even though they had fought, he had talked some sense into her. Maybe that luck would carry over to her audition.

The audition took place in a studio that was in the top floor of a brick warehouse-type building. JoJo arrived at seven o'clock sharp, handed a tall balding man—Bob, she presumed—her photo and résumé, and waited as he looked them over.

"Wonderful," he said, combing a hand through his nonexistent hair. "We're still waiting for the latecomers, but I want you to go over some of the script. It will give you some idea what I'm looking for. You should look at Eleanor."

It couldn't hurt when a director's first word after looking at your head shot was *wonderful*, JoJo thought hopefully. She clutched her script and ambled over to the place where about thirty other women of various ages and physical descriptions sat either reading the pages given to them or mentally going over the material they had prepared. JoJo sat in a folding chair, but as she read the first lines of her ten-page excerpt, a tiny frisson of panic networked its way across her nervous system.

ELEANOR: Franklin, I have tried so hard to be a good wife to you.
FRANKLIN: And are you not happy, pumpkin?
ELEANOR: Oh, I know most women would be satisfied to be living in the White House, but it's such a bummer sometimes.

Her panic attack became full-fledged as she flipped through the remaining pages. History had never been her best subject, but it didn't take a genius to figure out that she didn't have a prayer of being cast in this role. "This play is about Eleanor Roosevelt?" she asked aloud to no one in particular.

A woman looked up, gave JoJo's youthful appearance a once-over, smiled and shrugged. "They can do a lot with makeup."

"Not that much," JoJo said. And what could they do about the fact that Franklin Roosevelt was calling his wife *pumpkin?* She got up to confront Bob.

"It's going to be an avant-garde modern feminist approach," he told her, as if that explained why he had said that a twenty-three-year-old Italian girl would be wonderful auditioning for the part of Eleanor Roosevelt. Hadn't this man seen the Jane Alexander movie, or the films in high school? Eleanor Roosevelt was a tall, stocky patrician with buck teeth and a fluty voice.

She didn't even bother to mention that Eleanor Roosevelt was feminist and modern enough already without the help of some crackpot director. All she could think about was that shopping bag of food Peter had brought over to her apartment, and about what a terrible disappointment her first audition in months had turned into.

"Frankly," she said to Bob, "I can't see myself playing this any more than I could see Shannen Doherty playing Barbara Bush."

And that was the end of that.

"You mean you just walked out, without doing your monologue or anything?"

Sitting at the counter to Peter and Josh's kitchen, JoJo swallowed a bite of the crab crepe Josh had made earlier and stared at Peter incredulously. "What would have been the point?"

She had come straight over to the guys' apartment, feeling low and discouraged and in need of cheering up. After getting psyched up to perform, the reality of the audition had been a letdown, to say the least.

But more disappointing was the fact that Peter, apparently, had no intention of lifting her spirits.

"It would have been practice for you," he said.

"It would have been a waste of time."

"You might have gotten the part," Peter insisted.

"Please!" JoJo exclaimed. "I didn't have a chance."

"And even if she did," Josh put in, "would she have wanted to do a crazy modern play about Eleanor Roosevelt?"

"Exactly," JoJo agreed. "Which is what I told Bob."

"No, you didn't," Peter argued. "You made a snide remark about Barbara Bush."

"Well, he got my meaning."

Peter sent her a disapproving stare. Somehow, his glasses made him seem more stern, almost fatherly. "You probably really hacked the director off. You should have at least been more polite."

JoJo took a deep breath, trying to calm her nerves. She'd come here expecting some understanding. Instead, she was getting raked over the coals. "You weren't there. The guy was a loon."

"Yeah, but that loon might be directing something you'd be interested in actually being in one day, and how's he going to remember you now?"

Leave it to Peter the ex-business major to be concerned with networking at a time like this. "I doubt he'll remember me at all. I only talked to him for a minute." Didn't he understand that she was shaken up, and that his argumentative stance was doing nothing to help her nerves?

Peter shook his head slowly, almost mournfully. "Oh, well," he said with a sigh. "Maybe next time you'll think before you say something stupid."

JoJo felt her face heat up in anger. His high-handedness was too much, especially when it was because of him that she had run off hell-for-leather to the first audition she came across in the paper in the first place! He had her completely panicked about wasting her time; the least he could do was be a little nicer to her when his advice blew up in her face.

She was about to tell him so, too, in not-so-nice terms, when Josh said warningly, "Gee, bud, I don't think JoJo came here for a lecture."

JoJo sent him a grateful smile. At least there was one person in Chicago who would take her side. "Let's just drop it. It was just a disaster of an evening."

Peter was still shaking his head. "I still think Bob was right. You might have really spiced up old Eleanor."

Josh laughed, then, in a keen imitation of Eleanor's high warbly voice, he said, "Maybe sooo."

JoJo's mouth turned up in a smile. "You should have auditioned, Josh. I bet Bob would have loved *your* Eleanor Roosevelt."

"That would have been really avant-garde!" he agreed enthusiastically. "But, having seen him live on stage, I would have to say that Peter would be the better choice."

JoJo was shocked. "You never told me you'd acted before!"

Peter shrugged. "It was just in high school."

"Yeah, but it was *just* the biggest part in the biggest musical Newland High School ever performed!" Josh exclaimed.

"A musical?" Now this *was* interesting. Peter's face was turning red.

"Peter sang 'Some Enchanted Evening,'" Josh informed her. "It was really something."

"Something really awful, you mean," Peter corrected. "I've never been so embarrassed in my life."

Josh laughed. "Think of it this way. You've got a proven litmus test—if a woman can hear you sing that song and still say she loves you, you know she's telling the truth."

"I've got to hear this song!" JoJo cried.

"Oh, no," Peter said, shaking his head adamantly.

They never goaded Peter into performing, but after Josh's intervention in their argument, JoJo felt the tension between her and Peter take a back seat to the camaraderie of the three of them. Yet, even as she sat on the couch with Peter watching a therapeutic hour of "Nick at Night" followed by the evening news, she caught her mind wandering back to the conflict between them.

Why were she and Peter arguing all of a sudden, anyway? Before, they had always gotten along great. But ever since last Sunday night, she'd felt herself becoming more and more restless.

She looked across the room, at Josh, and wasn't surprised to find him looking back at her. They both quickly moved their glances toward the TV again, but that one moment of eye contact was enough to confirm JoJo's worst suspicions. Her gaze was straying—and finding a willing target. Had Peter sensed the attraction between her and Josh—and was that why he was picking little arguments with her?

As if reading her thoughts, at that moment Peter squeezed her hand. "Hey, Jo, are you still awake?"

She snapped to attention and turned to look at him. To her surprise, she found that they were snuggled together on the couch in their usual fashion which, given her thoughts of a moment before, suddenly made her feel as low as a worm. "I just zoned out, I guess."

"How could that be? The evening news is so riveting!" Josh exclaimed, forcing her to turn back to him. Josh loved to poke fun at the local newscasts. "After another twenty commercials, they might actually finally tell us the five-day forecast."

Peter, who was used to this routine, ignored him. "Are you staying the night?" he asked JoJo.

She thought for sure she could feel Josh's eyes on her, awaiting her answer with curiosity. She didn't dare look over in his direction. How could she stay over, feeling as mixed-up as she did? "No. In fact, I'd better get home."

"I'll walk you," Peter said, disappointment in his voice.

"I'll be okay," JoJo insisted. "It's not that late."

They debated the point, and Peter won. Much as JoJo wanted to get home and be by herself, she could hardly argue about being escorted to her door.

They walked half the way in silence. The streets were slushy with half-melted snow, and their feet made crunching sounds as they trudged side by side. JoJo could sense that Peter was trying to find a way to broach something with her.

Finally he asked, "You're still planning on coming to Wisconsin for Christmas, aren't you?"

JoJo's mother was going to Germany over the vacation to visit her brother. "I guess. I'm still invited, right?"

"Of course!"

She looked at him suspiciously. "Then of course I'm coming. Is something wrong?"

"I was going to ask you the same question." He sighed, then shook his head. "We're still okay, aren't we?"

JoJo wasn't sure what to say. She didn't want to stir up more trouble if the tension between them was going to pass with time. Yet she wanted to be honest, too. "I guess we're just going through a weird phase," she said.

Peter thought for a moment. "What kind of phase do you think we're in?"

"Well..." She took a deep breath, then admitted truthfully, "A restless phase, I think."

Peter frowned. "I see."

"I guess it will pass," JoJo said. "I think we've just been going along at the same speed for a long time now."

He looked at her, his brown eyes speculative behind his glasses. "So you think one of us should take decisive action?"

She shuddered. That could mean anything—including breaking up. She wasn't sure she wanted to consider that. "Maybe."

He nodded pensively. In his old tweedy coat and a huge orange, blue and white muffler his mother had made for him, he looked adorable. He caught her looking at him, smiled, and in a surprise move, he pulled her into his arms and gave her a kiss that made her toes curl. "Maybe we need to give this phase of ours a little push," he suggested.

She stared at him uncomprehendingly for a moment, still dazed from his sudden kiss, but by the time she thought to ask what he'd meant, he had already turned and was walking away with a little bounce in his step.

Of course, she thought as she let herself in to her building and headed up the stairs, Peter was always happiest when he had a problem to solve. He would probably spend the next days methodically searching for a formula to solve their troubled relationship. Unfortunately, JoJo feared one didn't exist.

Six

"Peter's in a meeting. Would you like to leave a message?"

JoJo felt her shoulders sag in disappointment as she put her hand against her ear to block out the traffic noise. She was downtown after an audition and had hoped that Peter could meet her during his lunch break. That is, if he didn't consider lunch breaks too frivolous. It seemed Peter was all work and no play these days.

"No message," she said. "Thanks."

She hung up the telephone and looked down the busy street. She didn't feel like going home quite yet. A half block away was a coffee shop and she automatically headed for it. Some caffeine might be just what she needed to perk up after yet another disastrous audition. Then, maybe in a half hour or so, she would try Peter again. The man had to eat sometime.

JoJo ordered a cappuccino—a double—and made her way to a table near the window. People-watching had always been one of her favorite pastimes, and today she decided she would indulge herself. She didn't even bother to take out the newspaper in her oversize suede purse; instead, she simply started staring out the window.

People streamed by. It was December now, so everyone was decked out in his or her heaviest coat—the street looked like a parade of wool and fur. Hats of all types perched on peoples' heads, and necks were swathed in mufflers and scarves against the city's famous bitter wind. JoJo caught

the reflection of herself in the window wearing a simple be-
ret and a large wool scarf Peter had given her for her birthday soon after they had met.

She took the hat off and ran a smoothing hand over her
hair. She'd gotten it under control this morning, but no
matter how many gallons of spray she dumped on it, black
curly tendrils would escape the confines of her neat French
braid. It had always been that way. In high school she'd
hated her curly hair and had tried everything to straighten
it. So desperately did she want a sleek page-boy cut like all
the other girls had that she finally shelled out a ton of the
money she had saved working after school to have her hair
chemically straightened. The procedure had transformed her
hair from curly to just plain kinky. When she finally got her
page-boy haircut, she looked like Larry from the Three
Stooges.

Remembering that disaster, she looked quickly back into
the window again to make sure that she didn't look *that* bad.
But when her eyes glanced up, she found herself face-to-face
with a pair of familiar blue eyes, staring straight at her. Josh
had his face pressed up against the glass and was smiling at
how distracted she'd been.

JoJo smiled back. It was great to see *somebody* she knew,
though the instant tripping of her heartbeat warned her that
this chance meeting might not be such a good thing.

Josh mouthed some words she couldn't catch, then ges-
tured with his gloved fingertip that he was going to join her.
JoJo quickly shook her head in an attempt to hold him off,
but he was already heading toward the door. The line for
coffee was short, and before long Josh was across from her,
shedding his coat, muffler and hat and sinking into the uncomfortable little iron chair on the other side of the round
marble-topped table.

*If you're going to have to people-watch just one person,
Josh isn't a bad choice,* she thought to herself as she stared

into his handsome face. Then she caught herself and turned away.

"Are you okay?" Josh asked, concerned. "You looked funny for a second."

JoJo glanced back at him nervously and took a quick swig of cappuccino. She wished now that she hadn't gotten such a large cup. She would be stuck here forever. "I'm fine," she said. "Did you just come from class?"

"Yeah. I can't wait to get a vacation."

He made it sound as if he'd been busting rocks all semester, instead of whipping up soufflés. Josh went to classes a lot, but it wasn't as though he were actually working to support himself at the same time, like most people were forced to. She almost reminded him of how lucky he was in that respect, then stopped herself. Was she turning into Peter?

"Are you still coming to Wisconsin at Christmas?" Josh asked.

The question startled her. "Why?" she returned. "Peter asked me the same thing."

Josh shrugged casually. "Oh, I don't know. Things between you and Peter seemed kind of... tense. I thought maybe you two were on the outs."

"Not at all." JoJo shook her head emphatically, though she feared the words were a lie. "And I'm still going to Wisconsin."

"My mother will be glad to see you."

At the mention of Barb, JoJo perked up. "She's so neat, Josh. I really loved talking to her over Thanksgiving."

"She thought you were pretty cool, too. In fact..." Josh reached behind him and pulled out his wallet. He rifled through his many credit cards and finally came up with what he was looking for—a scrap of paper with a name and a phone number scrawled across it. He handed it across the table to JoJo.

"My mother told me to give that man's name to you. He's some kind of acting teacher."

"Great!" JoJo exclaimed, looking at the torn sheet of paper with new interest, thinking smugly of Peter's warning that Barb would forget all about her promise. *Otto Kleist.* Then she remembered her disaster of this morning. "After the dreadful performance I gave this morning, I'm going to need all the wisdom Otto Kleist has to bestow on me."

Josh laughed. "You went on another audition already?"

"I've been on four in the past week and a half," JoJo said, feeling a little hurt that Peter hadn't bothered to tell Josh what she was up to.

"You're so industrious."

"Funny you should use that word. The part I auditioned for was for a character in an industrial film. And get this— it was going to be a training film for temporary workers. You know, to show new employees how to greet people and use a switchboard, and stuff like that."

"Sounds like it would be right up your alley."

JoJo let out a throaty laugh. "Not according to these people. First, they said I didn't *look* like a temp—especially not a receptionist. Can you believe that?"

"Haven't you heard? Only blondes answer phones," he joked.

JoJo rolled her eyes. "Apparently. I was so ticked off. Finally I bulldozed them into letting me read."

"What happened?"

This was so humiliating to admit. After a moment's hesitation, she blurted out, "I was terrible!"

"Terrible?" Josh asked.

"Terrible! I don't know what went wrong." She shook her head, still amazed at the way she had fallen apart. "All of the sudden, after making such a big stink about how well suited I was for the part, I sat down in front of that fake switchboard, and I just got so nervous. My hands were sweating so hard, I could barely hold on to the receiver. All I really had to say was 'Hello, may I help you?'—and I kept muffing the line!"

Josh shook his head. "Sounds like a bad case of the jitters."

"The jitters? It was a full-fledged panic attack!" She buried her head in her hands and moaned. "Oh, it's hopeless."

Josh reached across the table and patted her shoulder comfortingly. "Don't think that way! Everybody has a bad day every once in a while." He tapped a finger on the little scrap of paper he'd given her. "Call Otto. I bet he can help you with those nerves."

JoJo sent him a skeptical frown. "It's not as if he's the Wizard of Oz, Josh. I doubt that man can make me a good actress when I'm just not."

"Will you stop beating yourself up over this?" Josh said. "No one said you weren't a good actress. You just had a bad morning. Next time you'll be more prepared."

JoJo sighed. "Maybe so."

"I know so," he insisted. "Besides, Mom has an eye for these things, and she said you had a definite *presence.*"

"She did?" JoJo suddenly felt her depression lifting.

"Yeah." Josh took a sip from his coffee cup. "I don't know what it means, but she said you had it."

JoJo laughed. "I think your mother is so great. I can't wait to see her again."

"Good. She's coming to town sometime soon to do some Christmas shopping."

JoJo felt buoyed by the prospect. "When?"

Josh shrugged his shoulders. "Soon. That's as specific as she could get. Mom hates to make plans until the very last minute."

That wasn't very handy if she needed to take a day off, but JoJo was too excited to dwell on the inconvenience of Barb's quirks. Just the prospect of seeing her again made the future seem less bleak.

"Talking to your mother made me feel...confident," she said to Josh.

He nodded knowingly. "Mom loves talking to people. All the kids in high school used to think she was so cool, they always wanted her and my stepdad to be the chaperon parents at school dances." He smiled, remembering. "Of course, the principal and faculty always preferred *Peter's* parents."

JoJo cracked up. "I'll bet. They're the perfect PTA types."

"Are you kidding? Peter's mother *was* the PTA in Newland. She dedicated her life to bake sales and Monday-night meetings."

"I envy both of you." She loved her family, but sometimes she wished she could have had the small-town upbringing that Peter and Josh had. She wondered whether she would have turned out differently.

"Where did your mother grow up?" she asked Josh.

"New York. Long Island. I lived there, too, until she married my stepdad. But I was only four at the time, so I don't remember it too well."

JoJo took another sip of cappuccino. No wonder she felt an affinity to the woman—they'd grown up in the same place. Almost. "We lived in Manhattan. My father still does."

Josh frowned. "You don't go back there very often."

"My father isn't very pleasant to visit. He never quite got used to the responsibility of having kids, so he never knows what to do with my brother and me, even now that we're grown-up."

They drank their coffees in silence for a moment. There were more people on the sidewalk outside now as the time drew closer to lunch hour.

"I was going to call Peter," JoJo said, looking at her watch. She'd already been sitting for a half hour, and it seemed to her that Josh had just gotten there.

"Is something wrong?"

"No, I was hoping he'd have lunch with me."

"Peter?" Josh asked, raising his eyebrows in surprise. "He says he always eats at his desk."

"I thought it might make a nice change. Besides, I needed someone to talk to about my audition." She frowned. "Although maybe that wasn't such a good idea."

Josh regarded her with interest. "Why not?"

She shrugged, not sure how to find words for the uneasiness she felt inside. Maybe she shouldn't be talking to Josh about his best friend, but who else did she have to confide in? "I don't know. It's just . . . I don't think Peter has much patience with people who aren't sure how to go out and get what they want."

When Josh said nothing, she continued. "He found his job so quickly after college, and he's been moving steadily up. But it's not always that cut-and-dried when you're facing a career in the theater."

"Or in the restaurant business," Josh agreed.

"That's why it was so wonderful to talk to your mother. It was as if she understood my problems, while Peter can't see beyond the practical, problem-solving aspect. He thinks all I need to do is audition and audition, and something will turn up."

"He's right, in a way."

"But I need to be prepared, and right now I just don't feel that confident in myself. And auditioning when you're not ready doesn't do anything to boost your confidence, believe me."

To her relief, Josh nodded in understanding. "Pete's just got a different way of looking at things. I know he worries about you, though."

JoJo's mouth turned down. "That's just it," she said sadly. "He worries about me, but his response when I'm down is always to give advice. Sometimes I just want a shoulder to lean on."

"Are you down now?" Josh asked.

She smiled. "Actually, I was, but I feel better after talking to you."

"Great," Josh said. "Since you don't need Peter's shoulder to lean on, you can have lunch with me instead."

Her cup clattered down on her saucer and, with her napkin, she nervously dabbed at the coffee she'd spilled. "Oh, no, I couldn't."

"Why not? You don't have work today, and my classes are over until tomorrow."

How could she explain how traitorous to Peter she felt when she was with Josh, without completely giving away her feelings? "I only stopped in here in the first place to wait out a half hour to call Peter," she said.

"Oh." Josh looked disappointed for a second; then his face brightened. "So call him. We can all have lunch together. And if Peter's not available, you'll just have to put up with me."

He'd insinuated himself so cleverly into her plans that she'd look like a real pill if she refused now. Besides, he and Peter *were* best friends; it was only natural that they would all have lunch together.

If Peter was able to get away. She hoped he would be able to.

"That sounds fun," she said, fishing through the bottom of her purse for a quarter. "I'll just give him a call now."

There was a little phone booth near the door of the coffee shop, which she approached with trepidation. If Peter couldn't come to lunch, she'd have to spend another hour alone with Josh. On the other hand, Josh had been so great to talk to, she really wanted to spend more time with him. Maybe a tiny part of her even hoped that Peter *wouldn't* be able to make it.

She looked back at the table where Josh was sitting by himself, watching her. He smiled. She sent him a little wave, dialed the number and waited.

Glenda patched her through to Peter's phone, but after five rings the call rolled back over. "Sorry," the receptionist said crisply. "He's probably still in his meeting. Do you want to leave a message for him this time?"

She glanced at Josh, then out the window. She could give the name of a restaurant, and then, if he had time, Peter could meet them. But Glenda was so impatient, JoJo rationalized, and she hated long messages. And Josh was waiting, and she was hungry....

"Oh, just tell him JoJo called."

"Will do." The connection broke off, and JoJo replaced the phone in its cradle slowly. Surprisingly, she felt as though a weight had been taken off her shoulders. What harm could there be in having lunch with a friend?

She approached the table, smiling. "I guess it's just you and me," she told Josh.

He flashed her a devilish grin. "Then I know just what we should do," he said.

She wasn't sure whether she trusted the conspiratorial expression on his face. "What?"

"Rent our very favorite movies," he replied, as if it were the most obvious thing in the world, "and pick up our very favorite deluxe everything-on-it pizza on our way home."

She aimed a disapproving stare at him, but she was sorely tempted.

"What's wrong?" he asked innocently. "An afternoon of staring at a flickering screen would be just the thing to get your mind off this morning's tragedy. I'd even let you watch *The Bodyguard* for the three millionth time."

Her breath caught. She was more than tempted—she was absolutely won over. That movie was her weakness, and Josh was right. Spending an afternoon staring at Kevin Costner was just what the doctor ordered.

Especially if she were staring at Kevin Costner while sitting next to Josh.

They strolled home as if they had all the time in the world, talking and laughing as they went. Down the street from Josh and Peter's apartment they stopped for their movies. Josh, a Daniel Day-Lewis fan, picked up *The Last of the Mohicans*, which was a movie JoJo had also loved. She let him know with a look that she was on to him.

"I thought you said that was a girl movie," she said.

"I hereby declare this 'Be Kind to JoJo Day,'" he announced. "Today we watch nothing but your favorite movies and eat only your favorite foods."

JoJo laughed. "I like the sound of that. I think we should make it a weekly tradition."

"And don't forget you're supposed to reciprocate."

They munched on pizza and watched the period piece first. Then, after a short break, they went right to *The Bodyguard.* JoJo had seen the movie countless times, but she couldn't help being drawn into the romance. And by the time Whitney Houston was singing the movie's theme song, she was completely absorbed. Corny as it was, it always got to her.

It was late afternoon by the time their double feature was over. JoJo stretched and yawned. "I haven't had such a lazy, unproductive day since college," she said.

"Isn't it great?" Josh said.

JoJo laughed. "Yeah, it is." She sighed wistfully. "I wish I were as beautiful as Whitney Houston, and could sing as well."

"Uh-oh," Josh said. "The movie was supposed to cheer you up, remember?"

"I'm afraid it might take more than a movie. Over Thanksgiving Peter told me I would have to face reality. Unfortunately, reality is a little more bitter than I'd expected it to be."

Josh scooted closer to her on the couch. "That was just two weeks ago. Give yourself time."

She smiled gratefully, then said good-naturedly, "I still think time would go faster if I were as talented as Whitney Houston."

"I think you're plenty talented. And I know someone as pretty as you are can't remain undiscovered for long."

Her mouth dropped open in surprise. Josh thought she was pretty? His girlfriends usually looked like models! "Right," she said dismissively. "I forgot this was 'Be Kind to JoJo Day.'"

"I wasn't just being nice," Josh said in a low, husky voice that made her feel very, very uncomfortable. He took her hand in his and leaned close. "I meant it."

Her mouth felt dry. When she spoke, her voice came out as a whispery croak. "I'd better go home."

"Why?"

"It's after four o'clock." She looked into his blue eyes. They were separated only by inches, and she could feel the warmth from his body as he leaned even closer to her. "I need to get back to my apartment and—"

He cut off her words with a light brushing of his lips against hers. The kiss was brief—barely a kiss at all, really—yet it sent a shock wave through her entire system. As if by instinct, she put her hand against his shoulder, and in response she felt him move his arm around her waist.

For a moment they simply looked into each other's eyes, just as they'd been doing for weeks now. JoJo suddenly wondered if he really had kissed her at all, or if the wonderful warm feeling coursing through her was only a response to something she had imagined. She had to find out.

This time, she leaned forward and tested his lips herself, gently at first. Then, as his hold around her waist tightened, she found herself pressing up against him, moving her hand to the back of his neck and pulling him down to her. She opened her mouth and they deepened the kiss. Lightning heat shot through her body as they touched and tasted and experimented in the feel of something so totally new.

It had been two years since she'd kissed anyone besides Peter....

At the thought of his name, JoJo took in a shocked breath. What was she doing? She pulled her mouth away from Josh's and pushed against his chest to disentangle herself from his arms. Josh was less muscled than Peter, but he was surprisingly strong, and he obviously was not as bothered by what they were doing as she was.

"Josh, please."

"What?"

"What do you think?" she cried, distressed. "I can't believe I just did that!"

"I can, Jo," he said in a surprisingly gruff voice. "It's all I've been able to think about for weeks now."

She stopped pushing against him and simply stared, dumbfounded. For all her angsting about Josh, it never occurred to her that he might be suffering sleepless nights, too. He leaned forward to kiss her again, and she ducked her head just in time. "But why?" she asked.

He kept her hand in his. "I've had a crush on you for months. I thought for sure you'd noticed." He examined her face closely. "I also thought you were beginning to feel the same way about me."

"I—" JoJo aimed her gaze away from him. Her face felt as though it were on fire. What had she gotten herself into? "I can't—" Her words cut off as she searched frantically for the right thing to say. "What about Peter?"

Josh released a deep breath, then finally let go of her hand. "Peter," he said—almost as if he had forgotten about him.

They sat side by side, their breaths slowly returning to normal. Finally JoJo admitted, "I guess I did sort of have a crush on you, too, but..."

"But I'm Peter's best friend," he finished for her.

She nodded miserably. "I feel so terrible!"

"Don't," Josh told her. "It's my fault, I guess. I sensed that you and Peter were having a hard time. I thought maybe the two of you were washed up."

"But even if we were, I still wouldn't want to come between the two of you," JoJo told him. "You guys have been friends for years."

"It wouldn't have to end our friendship."

For a moment, JoJo stared at him, uncomprehending. "What?" she asked. Did he mean his friendship with her—or with Peter?

He smiled. "It's not the end of the world, you know. Peter stole my girlfriend in seventh grade."

Seventh grade? "But Peter and I have been going out for two years."

"You're right. Jeopardizing my friendship with Peter would be nuts." He considered for a moment, then said, "But if we're careful, Peter doesn't even have to find out."

She looked anxiously at Josh. "What do you mean—find out about the kiss?"

"That, too. But if we want to take things further—"

JoJo launched herself off the couch in a split second. "Further! We can't!"

Josh laughed. "I seem to have hit a nerve."

Was it prudish not to want to cheat on your boyfriend? JoJo wondered suddenly. Josh seemed to be treating this all so casually, as if it were no big deal.

"We're both adults, Jo. People can't help being attracted to each other."

"I know that, but that doesn't mean we have to give in to our impulses."

He stood, too, and combed a hand through his longish hair in a frustrated gesture. "But sometimes, if you don't give in, they just build and build and build."

Obviously. Things had already built to the point that she was impulsively kissing him on the couch a mere hour before Peter was due to arrive home. She truly had lost her senses.

"I think we would be great together," Josh went on when she didn't speak. "It's not as if we would have to go steady, or something dopey like that."

JoJo's eyes widened in astonishment. "I can't cheat on Peter, Josh. Period. I'm just not the type to have…affairs." Affairs! The word sounded ridiculous even coming out of her mouth. Older people, sophisticated people in movies, had affairs. She'd never felt younger or more foolish than she did at this moment.

And she'd never seen Josh look more hurt.

"I really like you, Jo," he said. "I wouldn't want to pressure you into doing something you thought was wrong."

She nodded, straining to understand his point of view. "You're just more daring than I am, I guess."

He sent her a sad, crooked smile. "I really didn't mean to step out of line. I thought the feeling was mutual."

Unfortunately, it was more mutual that JoJo cared to admit. "We'll just have to forget the whole thing happened," she told him.

"That's not going to be very easy."

No, it wasn't. Unfortunately, she feared that for a long time to come she would remember how tenderly Josh had kissed her. She started making her way toward the door, gathering up her purse, coat, scarf and hat as she went. "Time takes care of most things." The trite words sounded flat and emotionless as they came out of her mouth.

His lips quirked up at the corners. "Don't worry, Jo. It won't happen again. Unless you want it to."

Somehow, those last words failed to comfort her. What she wanted was what worried her most of all. JoJo smiled nervously. "I'll see you later," she assured him just before she rushed out the door.

She sagged with relief when she made it out to the street, almost surprised to see the world going about its business as usual. The tempo of the quiet afternoon was completely out of sync with the way she felt. Her limbs felt boneless and quivery, as though she had Jell-O jiggling through her veins.

She made her way slowly down the sidewalk, focusing her mind solely on putting one foot in front of the other, trying her hardest not to think about Josh. But of course that was impossible. She couldn't forget his unbelievable words—*I've had a crush on you for months*. Why did she find them so hard to believe?

The privacy of her apartment was more welcome to her than ever before. She changed into jeans and a warm sweater, popped in an old tape into her tape deck and soon found herself relaxing to Sting's soothing voice. He was one of the few rock artists she and Peter could agree on, and in an odd way listening to him now made her feel as though she were already patching things up between them. Which was silly, considering that Peter was unaware of what had happened between her and Josh this afternoon.

And always would be, she hoped.

She lay down wearily on the futon and tried to clarify things in her mind. On the surface, the facts were easy to sort out. She loved Peter. She didn't love Josh. Unfortunately, her feelings didn't feel so cut-and-dried.

Maybe, she thought, if she repeated it to herself, her fuzzy confused feelings would clear up. *I love Peter,* she thought determinedly, just before she dropped off to sleep. *Don't I?*

Seven

The pounding was loud and insistent. JoJo bolted up on the futon and looked around her dark apartment, disoriented. What was going on?

There was another loud knock on her door—that was what had awakened her. She turned on a lamp and stepped into a pair of flats that she had shed by the coffee table.

"Hey, JoJo, it's me!"

JoJo froze. "Peter?" Suddenly the whole episode from that afternoon replayed through her mind, and she once again felt feverish and panicky. What was Peter doing here? Oh, Lord, had he talked to Josh? Did he know what had happened?

"Yes, it's Peter—that's who me is!" he hollered through the door.

He didn't sound particularly angry. Warily, she undid the night latch and opened the door.

Peter was standing in the hallway, his arms loaded down with flowers and a bottle of champagne. "Surprise!" he yelled, a goofy exuberant grin on his face.

She stared at him, stupefied, and desperately tried to shift gears. She'd expected anger—and she was faced with jubilation.

"Aren't you going to invite me in?"

She stepped aside, and looked down at her watch. It was six-thirty. "I must have fallen asleep."

"Yeah, I guess so," Peter said, laughing. "Your hair is smashed on one side. You sure are having a lazy day—Josh said you two watched movies all afternoon!"

"You talked to Josh?" JoJo asked, running to the bathroom to get a brush for her hair.

"Uh-huh, for a little bit. He told me that you had tried to call me to meet for lunch. Sorry, I didn't get your message until late this afternoon." He suddenly appeared in the door to the bathroom. JoJo caught his secretive smile in the mirror. "You want to know why?" he asked.

"Glenda said you were in a meeting."

"With my boss, and Personnel," he said.

The muscles in JoJo's face went slack, and she pivoted in shock. "Oh, no, Peter—you couldn't have been fired!"

"Not fired," he said, laughing. He picked her up, stepped back out into her room and twirled her around before setting her back on her feet. "I was promoted!"

JoJo smiled happily in relief. "That's terrific!" she said, giving him a big hug. "Why didn't you call me?"

"I did, but you weren't home, and I didn't leave a message because I wanted to tell you in person." He stepped back and did a little dance step. For the first time, JoJo noticed that he was wearing his spiffiest suit, including a tie she had given him last Christmas. "So what do you say? Let's celebrate!"

"Definitely," she agreed. "But I'm a wreck, and you look all dressed up."

"Of course! I made seven-thirty reservations at a great restaurant on Dearborn Street."

"That's a hike." It didn't give her much time to prepare, either.

"Wear heels. We can take a cab," he said. "We're rich!"

"*We* are?" she asked, still bowled over by his crazy mood.

"I was made a manager in accounting, which means a whopping eight-percent raise." Suddenly his face lost its animation and he pushed his glasses up on his nose. "Of course, I'm going to increase the amount I'm putting into retirement, so it's not going to *seem* like eight percent."

JoJo laughed and gave him a quick hug. "What a relief to hear you talking about things like pension benefits again. For a minute there I thought you had completely lost your head."

He shrugged, as though he couldn't help himself. "In my own small way, I have. At least for tonight. I have the un-conquerable urge to go spend a ridiculous amount of money in a very short time."

JoJo saw the roses he'd laid on the coffee table and picked them up. She felt a pang of guilt. While she and Josh had been kissing, Peter had probably been thinking about buy-ing these for her. "I need to put these in water," she said.

He took them from her. "I'll do it so you can get dressed. Just point me to a vase."

She pulled a tall glass container from her kitchen cabi-nets. "This should work," she told him and was sidestep-ping past him on her way out of the tiny kitchen when he pulled her to him again.

"I would be the happiest man alive if you wore that blue velvet dress of yours with the low neckline," he said.

JoJo swallowed, feeling another pang of guilt. "Okay."

"The champagne I brought is for later. I know it's a work night, but I thought, what the hell."

She laughed, attempting levity. "You only live once."

"It's okay if I stay over, isn't it?" JoJo nodded mutely in response. "Great," he said.

JoJo rushed out of the kitchen, grabbed her blue dress from the closet, then locked herself in the bathroom to dress. The tiny room felt claustrophobic, but she desper-ately needed to be alone for a moment to gather her wits. She couldn't believe Peter's timing. Surprising her like this wasn't like him at all; of course, it had been work that had spurred this spontaneity, not a sudden burst of love.

But maybe it was better this way, she lectured herself. Going out and having a good time with Peter was probably just what she needed to put the whole weird episode with Josh behind her. And wasn't this just a confirmation of why she loved Peter? He was a generous, hardworking guy who was going places. What woman wouldn't be crazy for him?

The restaurant they went to specialized in midwestern recipes done to perfection—a five star meat-and-potatoes place that naturally Peter would love. He ordered a huge steak and looked about the happiest man alive.

JoJo felt better being out with him.

For a little while.

"So what happened at the audition?" Peter asked her, once they were settled in and he'd explained all about his new position. "You haven't even mentioned it."

After everything else that had happened, she'd forgotten about the audition completely. "It didn't go so well."

Peter sighed lightly in commiseration. "Oh, well. Maybe next time. Hey, did I tell you I'm going to have an office now? A *real* office. It doesn't have a window, of course, but..."

JoJo smiled and tried without much success to focus on what Peter was saying, telling herself that it was only normal that he would be wrapped up in his big promotion. She didn't want to be petty. At the same time, her mind was tallying up the number of times he'd been equally dismissive of her problems before—times when he didn't have his promotion as an excuse.

Had it always been this way, or was she just being overly sensitive? She remembered when they'd first met, she had thought he was incredibly supportive. But of course, things were always great in the beginning of a relationship. That was why it was important not to rush into things.

She thought about how tempting it would be to rush into something with Josh. Josh was understanding. Of course, he was also, in Peter's words, a bounder. But would he dump on someone he really cared about?

Josh had truly been understanding when she was talking to him about her audition. And he'd looked so distraught when she broke off their kiss and told him there was no way things could continue between them. He must care for her at least a little, beyond just wanting to sleep with her....

"JoJo?"

Peter's voice broke through her distraction and, chagrined by her turn of thoughts, she focused on him. "What?"

"The waiter put your food in front of you five minutes ago and you haven't touched it." He took her hand in his and pressed it cautiously. "Are you sick?"

His face was filled with worry for her, and she felt herself flush in shame. "I'm fine," she assured him. To prove it, she retracted her hand, picked up her fork and took a bite of lamb. "It's delicious," she said.

He seemed satisfied, and returned to his steak. "I think there might be some problems in the accounting department...."

Usually, JoJo loved hearing office scuttlebutt. Not tonight, though. She was too confused. She'd been attached to Peter so long, it seemed weird to suddenly have developed an attachment to someone else. And yet, on the surface at least, Josh was so much more compatible with her personality.

How could she be so in love with one person, and yet be attracted to another?

Peter couldn't decide what kind of ring JoJo would like. By nature she was a flamboyant person, yet he couldn't see her wearing a diamond boulder on her finger every single day. Besides, he couldn't afford a boulder. But he wanted to get her something more than a solitary little chip. It was so hard to decide. He'd never guessed how many different settings there were for engagement rings.

He'd come into the jewelry store on impulse, which wasn't normal for him at all. But all morning he'd been sitting in his new office, not attending to his new work; instead he'd been doing more important figures. Annual income and expenditures for a family of three—true, there were only two of them right now, but he wanted to be prepared for any possibility. With his new raise, he could manage it pretty comfortably. They just wouldn't be able to have too many dinners out like the one they'd had the other night.

He frowned, remembering how distracted JoJo had seemed that night. It was almost as if she were unable to focus on what monumental changes this promotion could bring about for both of them. Finally, they would be able to get married and start building toward something lasting. Maybe start a family someday. He wouldn't even mind having kids right away.

But only when Jo was ready. He knew she had her own career to worry about. And yet, wouldn't it be better for her if she weren't always scraping to make ends meet? She managed to do pretty well with her temporary work, but she had no benefits, no retirement....

He caught himself before his mind could wander down the long and winding road of IRA's and life insurance, and he looked at his reflection in the glass case containing a mint of diamonds and other jewels. Did he really just think in terms of finances? Is that why JoJo had seemed so disinterested lately?

He thought about the jokes Josh and JoJo always made about him. Peter Lattimore, Mr. Straight Arrow. Mr. Plan Ahead. Mr. Nine-to-Five. He'd always laughed off his reputation as a future stuffed shirt of America. Now the idea made him shudder. Was that how JoJo really saw him?

He remembered how he'd dominated the conversation at dinner the week before, yacking away about percentage increases and the challenges of management. Suddenly he felt like the world's biggest fool. What did those mundane things mean to Jo, especially when her own dreams were faltering?

The problem was that her goals were so different from his. Frankly, he didn't quite understand why someone would want to dedicate her life to such a risky business as theater. Good and bad was such a subjective matter in acting, and to someone who loved security like he did, the chanciness of it all was a nightmare. He was nervous on her behalf. To him, it would be akin to throwing all your money into penny stocks. There was no guaranteed payoff.

Risk, securities, pay-offs. Peter's face in the glass turned a shade paler, and a bead of sweat formed at his temple. Good grief, he couldn't stop himself!

Josh and JoJo were right—everything was always plan, plan, plan with him. He didn't have a spontaneous bone in his body. The other night he'd patted himself on the back for going out on the spur of the moment, but it had been to a restaurant they had been to several times, and he'd still managed to make reservations. And once they were there, he'd probably bored her to tears with all of his shop talk.

Was JoJo bored with him?

He'd been so preoccupied with work lately because he'd sensed he was on the verge of moving up. But he'd never wanted to move up alone. Without JoJo, promotions and savings accounts and retirement benefits didn't mean a whole lot to him. She was the one he was supposed to be sharing a rocking chair with. He was totally, completely head over heels in love with her.

Maybe he hadn't been demonstrative enough, or supportive enough. His way of trying to help her had been to attempt to light a fire under her—which had certainly gotten her moving, auditionwise. She'd gone on more calls in the weeks since Thanksgiving than she had during the previous two years. Unfortunately, she'd met with some bad luck, and since that terrible drive home from Wisconsin, he hadn't been much of a sympathetic ear. He'd left the pep talks to others, like Josh.

What a dolt! Why should he be leaving Josh the job of cheering up his girlfriend? That was one of the more important parts of a relationship, after all.

He needed to think more about just being there for JoJo, he decided. Maybe if they were married, and together more, this would be easier. For one thing, JoJo would be released from the stress of having to go out on auditions after spending a day in some strange office. Best of all, they would have more time together. There would be none of the hassle of your-place-or-my-place... just about fifty or so years of cohabiting. That was definitely an idea that appealed to him.

Christmas. He would ask her at Christmas.

Would she be surprised? He remembered the look on her face at Thanksgiving when his family had been joking with them about getting married. But surely she'd just been embarrassed—who wouldn't have been? His family could be pretty overpowering at times, but it wouldn't be so bad once she was one of them.

Christmas. It was only two weeks away.

Happiness surged through him. He was turning over a new leaf. Today he was going to start being Mr. Spontaneous. Mr. Warmth and Understanding. Mr. Spur-of-the-Moment.

"Have you made up your mind, sir?"

Peter looked up at the clerk who had greeted him when he'd come into the store. He'd been standing in front of the same case for a long time now, lost in thought, so it was no wonder the clerk assumed he must have reached some kind of conclusion. Any normal person would have.

But *he* wasn't normal. Not anymore. As JoJo's husband-to-be, even if she didn't know it yet, he was definitely a cut above the humdrum crowd. And just to prove it, he decided to do something extremely spontaneous, some might even say foolhardy.

"How much is this emerald?" The beautiful green stone was surrounded by a cluster of little diamonds on each side. It was gorgeous and unique, perfect for Jo. He was practically giddy with anticipation.

The clerk named an exorbitant price that made Peter flinch. It wasn't *that* nice. Impulse buying was all very fine and good, but he didn't want to get rooked!

Besides, he had until Christmas to buy the ring.

"How about this sapphire?"

It was cheaper, but he wasn't very excited by it, especially when he remembered where he'd seen it before. It was very similar to Princess Diana's engagement ring. No wonder it was marked down—look how her marriage had turned out!

He pointed at rings and haggled with the clerk for a half hour, then decided he would never find anything he liked so much as that emerald. Still, he couldn't bring himself to pull out his Visa card. It just wasn't prudent not to shop around for such a considerable purchase.

Becoming Mr. Spontaneity was apparently going to take some practice.

Where had Peter gone off to?

JoJo was, as her mother would always say, fit to be tied. Whatever that meant. Barb had called the day before to tell them she was coming into town the next day and to invite them all out to lunch. They decided to wait until she actually made it to Chicago to firm up plans, so JoJo had told Peter to stand by and she would call him at the office so he could meet them.

She had received Barb's call from the train station thirty minutes ago, however, and now Peter was nowhere to be found. Glenda, sounding more miffed than usual, said that he'd stepped out at eleven-thirty and hadn't returned. It was very unlike him, and very inconvenient.

This was not a good time for Peter to have gone AWOL, JoJo fumed as she put the phone back in its cradle. Now she would have to face dealing with Josh alone. Of course Barb would be there, and she looked forward to seeing her, but it was going to be awkward, given what had happened between Josh and herself.

That wasn't Peter's fault... but she still managed to blame him for the discomfort she felt about the whole situation. The only time he'd thought to pay attention to her lately— their dinner together the other night—it was to celebrate *his* job. He was becoming a complete workaholic, and she was playing an increasingly smaller part in his life.

Worse, Peter appeared oblivious to the fact that things were disintegrating between them. She'd given him only the vaguest of reassurances that night he'd walked her home, and since that time he'd been acting as if everything were hunky-dory. He hadn't even noticed how jittery she'd been the other night. Couldn't he see how she felt about his best friend? She had been walking around for days afraid that the whole world could read her attraction in her face.

Maybe she was a better actress than she thought!

She went to her closet and pulled out an old skirt from the sixties that she had bought at a secondhand store; it was black and had a heavy brocade pattern stitched into it. Over this she wore a long red pullover and finished off with tights and a pair of low pumps. The effect was cute, but not too dressy. They were only having a casual lunch at a small neighborhood restaurant.

After running a quick brush through her hair and tying it back with a silky black scarf—Barb would probably go for that—she inspected her appearance in the mirror, feeling oddly nervous. More makeup. She threw some on, telling herself she wanted to make a good impression on Barb.

She met Josh and Barb at Josh's apartment. Barb looked sophisticated in a long navy cape over a casual wool dress. And Josh, of course, was dressed in his usual eclectic style, with jeans, a dress shirt and the most brightly printed tie JoJo had ever seen. The tie with parrots all over it was obviously a concession to having lunch with his mom—probably Barb had brought it back for him from one of her vacations. He looked fantastic, as usual.

Both were surprised to see her alone. "Will Peter be meeting us at the restaurant?" Barb asked.

JoJo shook her head, trying to tamp down her irritation. "I don't know where he went. Yesterday he said he was looking forward to lunch, but today he disappeared from the office."

"I hope nothing bad happened to him."

To her shame, JoJo realized that this possibility hadn't occurred to her. But wouldn't he have called her by now if something was wrong? "I'm sure he's okay. He's been sort of preoccupied lately."

"Sort of?" Josh said. "He's turning into Mr. Nose-to-the-Grindstone."

So Josh had noticed, too, JoJo noted.

"That's too bad," Barb said sincerely. "I'd hate to see Peter fall into the trap of so many men who can't seem to leave their work behind at the office."

"It's getting him to leave the office that's the hard part," Josh said.

"Well he's obviously out of there now," JoJo threw in as an attempt at levity. "No one can find him."

They headed out to the restaurant, which was a quiet, out-of-the-way place perfect for an intimate lunch with old friends. Of course, Barb was actually a new friend, but to JoJo it seemed as if they had an easier rapport than she had with some people she had known for years.

"I called your friend Otto," she told Barb. "He sounded so nice. He said I could join a group of people he works with every Monday."

"That's wonderful!" Barb said. She couldn't have been more pleased, and launched into a story about herself and Otto when they were working at a dinner theater together in the seventies.

JoJo listened intently. She had never even seen Otto Kleist—she'd only spoken to him that once on the phone—but from Barb's conversation she could tell that he was a corpulent man with a deep voice and a wicked sense of humor. During a dinner scene he and Barb were having on stage during one production, he'd replaced the real food Barb was supposed to eat with plastic.

"Of course we were little more than kids back then—very prone to breaches of professionalism."

"Mom, you were *thirty* when that happened," Josh said, shooting JoJo a long-suffering-son look.

In that instant, their gazes met and held. Suddenly JoJo's cheeks felt as if they were on fire, and her throat was parched. She reached across her plate for her water glass and nearly knocked it over.

"When you're thirty you'll think you're little more than a kid, too, I assure you," Barb said. She glanced over at JoJo and frowned. "Dear, are you all right? Your face is splotchy."

"It's hot in here all of a sudden," JoJo said weakly. "Don't you think so?"

Barb struck a match to light her long skinny cigarette and looked around the place with a puzzled air. "I hadn't noticed."

"I had," Josh said, once again capturing her gaze. Was it a gift, or was he being so sexy on purpose?

JoJo couldn't believe her lack of concentration. One minute she'd been perfectly focused on Barb and her story, and in the next she was completely distracted by Josh. What was the matter with her?

Unfortunately, she knew the answer to that. Lust, pure and simple.

"What else have you done recently?" Barb asked.

Kissed your son was the thought that immediately popped into JoJo's mind. She struggled to come up with a less embarrassing answer. "Oh, I've been doing quite a few auditions," she said, unable to keep her fingers from nervously knotting the ends of the tablecloth. "Nothing very promising. Yesterday I auditioned to do voice-overs for a baby-food commercial and a shoe-store chain."

"Somehow, when I hear your voice, I don't usually think of strained vegetables," Josh said jokingly.

"I hope someone does," JoJo said, keeping her eyes trained away from him. "I could use the money."

Barb exhaled and regarded JoJo through a veil of smoke. "Voice-overs can be quite lucrative. You're a smart girl."

Once again, the smile Barb bestowed upon JoJo made her feel as if she were the only actress in the world who had ever thought to audition for a commercial. Her spirits lifted, and she took a sip of the wine in the glass in front of her. The three of them were sharing a bottle.

"I'd heard that commercials could make a lot of money, but I'm basically trying for anything I can."

"Oh, yes, by all means," Barb said, "do as much as you can. But don't become so wrapped up in acting that you forget the more important things life has to offer."

JoJo couldn't think of anything more important than acting. Just look at how she'd reacted when she'd become discouraged after moving to Chicago—her self-esteem was in the basement. Now that she was out pounding the pavement again, she felt better about herself, more confident, even if the results she'd been getting were less than spectacular. That as much as anything proved to her how integral her chosen profession was to her happiness.

"I've seen women and men make foolish mistakes," Barb continued, "choosing to put their personal lives on hold until they've 'made it big'—even when they realize how few people actually do that."

"You were successful," JoJo said.

"I made a good living," Barb admitted. "And even so, I never found the satisfaction on a stage that I found in sleepy Newland, Wisconsin, raising Joshua."

"Gee, Mom, I'm touched," Josh said, with a hint of sincerity managing to poke through his wry humor.

Barb reflected for a moment then let out a throaty laugh. "Of course, raising a child was more of a challenge. I was a *ghastly* housewife. Still am. Poor Joshua had to learn to cook because I couldn't, I'm afraid."

His face broke out in a wide grin. "You see? All those burned meals paid off. They pointed me toward a profession."

They laughed as their lunches were placed before them. Conversation during the meal consisted chiefly of hometown gossip for Josh's benefit since he had missed coming home at Thanksgiving, but Barb delivered it with such a flair that JoJo was drawn into the infidelities, rivalries and even the schoolboard squabbles of Newland, Wisconsin.

"I can't believe such a small town has such a large amount of trouble going on."

"Oh, dear, we've got more 'going on' than 'Melrose Place.' When I married Josh's stepfather, I moved from a fictional soap opera into a real one!" Barb said. She went on to relate the story of a couple who had been married twelve years when it was discovered the wife had been having an affair with her high school sweetheart the whole time.

"The *whole* time," Barb said, shaking her head in disbelief. "And *I* never suspected a thing. Neither did the husband, which is almost as surprising."

For weeks, JoJo had wondered how Barb had managed to give up what she considered a glamorous profession for a decidedly unglamorous life in a tiny city like Newland. Now she knew. Everything fascinated Barb. She found the littlest events of the day interesting and worth talking about—and embellishing.

"Nothing that interesting going on here in Chicago, is there, Jo?" Josh asked.

She laughed. "Not that I know of, unfortunately."

"Don't you believe it!" Barb said. "The only difference between here and there is you don't know your neighbors. But I bet if you examined the lives around you that you do know, you'd find some pretty steamy conflict going on." She looked pointedly from one of them to the other.

Josh and JoJo's smiles disappeared, and the table fell suddenly silent. JoJo took one last bite of the sandwich she'd ordered, then pushed her plate away. Suddenly her appetite was gone.

She didn't want to look Josh in the eye, but she couldn't avoid it, either. He was irresistible to her for some reason—as if he were a magnet and she were an insubstantial little paper clip who couldn't resist his pull. But she had to resist.

Or at least try.

"Excuse me," JoJo said, placing her napkin on the table. "I'll be back in a moment."

Barb flashed her a curious smile before JoJo turned to weave her way toward the rest rooms. Too much wine, JoJo told herself. Too much Josh.

Eight

"Joshua!" Barb cried.

Josh tore his gaze from watching JoJo walk away and looked at his mother. "Yeah?"

"Isn't JoJo wonderful?" she asked.

He laughed. "I know she is, Mom."

"It seems to me that you two would get along like gangbusters."

"We do," Josh replied. "That's why she's my friend."

"*Just* your friend?"

Warning bells went off in Josh's head. He'd seen his mother try to play matchmaker before. "*Just* friends, Mom," he said.

She sat back in her chair and lit another cigarette thoughtfully. Finally, after her little fire ritual was finished, she shook her head adamantly. "I don't believe it."

"Mom..."

"I've seen what's going on between you two!" Barb cried. "You can hardly keep your eyes off each other."

"But that doesn't mean anything's going on, as you put it."

"It's usually a fairly certain sign."

"JoJo is Peter's girlfriend," Josh reminded her. "Remember Peter? That kid next door who always made good grades? The fellow who just happens to be my best friend?"

Barb frowned. "That is an obstacle."

"It's more than that, Mom. It means JoJo is strictly off-limits. Absolutely nothing will happen between her and me."

"Whose decision was that?" Barb inquired.

Josh frowned. "Both of ours," he lied, not wanting to admit that, when it came to JoJo, he was willing to fudge on his principles.

Barb arched a knowing brow at him and leaned close. "Because if it was JoJo's, I think she might have changed her mind."

That statement caught Josh's attention. "Why would you think that?" he asked, feigning only mild interest.

"Because she's been smoldering during the whole meal, sweetheart. Both of you have. I doubt either of you has heard a word I've said the whole time!"

"That's not true," Josh told her. Sometimes it was hard to tell with his mom. She loved drama so much that often she attempted to stir some up where there was none.

"All right, maybe I'm exaggerating. But I know I'm right, darling. The looks JoJo has been sending you don't lie."

Was his mother right? After their kiss, JoJo had seemed so certain that she wanted nothing to do with him anymore. They were supposed to forget the kiss ever happened, she had told him. Maybe she hadn't been able to forget any more than he had.

Or maybe this all was tied up in whatever was going on with her and Peter. He still wasn't sure he wanted to step into the middle of their problems. "I think she and Peter are going through a bad patch," Josh told his mother.

"It seems to me that Peter has practically abandoned the poor girl."

Josh thought for a moment. It did seem that way sometimes, but he knew it wasn't true. Was it? If he and JoJo were going to split, it opened up a whole new set of possibilities.

"I think you and JoJo would be perfect together," Barb declared. "And it's obvious you're crazy about each other."

"I don't know if I'd say crazy," Josh said. "I was never even that attracted to JoJo that much until..."

His words trailed off and Barb's blue eyes narrowed in on him like a shot. "Aha! So you admit you're attracted to her?"

Josh shrugged haplessly. "Who wouldn't be? She's pretty and talented and has a great personality. She does a great Julia Child impression, even."

"Then I guess she's got everything," Barb said, who sometimes became exasperated with her son's flippant attitudes. "She would be perfect for you, Josh. You need someone permanent in your life."

"Permanent?" Josh practically shuddered at the word.

"You can't run around being playboy of the western world forever."

Josh pretended innocent surprise. "I can't?"

Barb laughed. "You're just like your father!" Then she frowned. "That's not a compliment, you know."

He ducked his head. "I know."

"There are advantages to growing up, Josh. Responsibility isn't a complete drag, as you would say."

"I know, I know, I know." Josh looked at his mother and said, "I swear, Mom, I don't want to be like my dad, the kind of guy who can't even stick with one woman for a year. I really admire the life-style you have with David. But I just don't think I'm ready for that yet."

"Does JoJo feel the same way?"

"I don't know. What difference does it make?"

"Because underneath her mod exterior, I have the feeling she's a girl harboring some traditional desires."

"Maybe," Josh said.

"I would hate to think you were leading her on, Josh. She deserves better than that, especially if she's having problems with Peter."

Josh frowned. "What does that have to do with me?"

"If JoJo thinks you appreciate her in ways Peter doesn't, that could influence her actions."

Josh shook his head. It was all too muddled and complicated for his taste. To his way of thinking, if a man and woman were attracted to each other, that should be all that mattered. Though he knew JoJo had a few more qualms than he had, she was a big girl and could make her own decisions.

"I'm not leading her on," he said finally, sorting things out for himself as he spoke. "It's up to her if she wants to get involved—I've told her that much."

Barb's mouth turned down in a thoughtful frown. "I'm afraid she may want too many things at once," she said, shooting her son a quelling glance. "And I'm afraid you're going to take advantage of that."

"Me?" He raised his eyebrows innocently. "I think I've helped JoJo lately. I've certainly spent a lot more time with her than Peter has."

Barb laughed, intentionally misinterpreting his remark. "You think your flirting with her has made her feel better about herself?"

Josh smiled in return. "I hadn't thought of it that way, but yeah, I guess being around me has boosted her ego. I have that effect on women."

"My dear boy, you are shameless," Barb said in her husky voice. "And you've got a whole lot to learn."

"Which is precisely why I don't want to settle down," Josh told her. "Why should some poor girl have to be my test case?"

A moment later JoJo was back in her seat. "Sorry I was so long," she said, smiling. She looked as if she had composed herself again, Josh noticed, which was more than he could say for himself.

"I hope you two have the afternoon free," Barb said.

JoJo glanced up anxiously. "Did you need help with something?"

"Of course! Shopping alone is no fun."

JoJo thought about the pumps she had thrown on and groaned inwardly. They definitely weren't good shopping shoes.

Barb smiled. "And then I thought you two could treat me to something touristy, like a trip to the museum."

This JoJo couldn't resist. The Art Institute of Chicago had some of the greatest paintings in the world, and she loved to hang out there.

"We can go there after shopping and have coffee," Barb suggested.

"Sounds fun," Josh said. "How about you, JoJo? Are you game?"

She looked into his blue, blue eyes and considered for a moment. The longer she stayed around Josh, the weaker her defenses became. Originally she had expected that she would be with Peter, and that his having to go back to work would give her an opportunity to disentangle herself if she needed it. There wasn't an easy out now.

On the other hand, what else did she have to do? If she went back to her apartment, she would probably go stir-crazy. Since she had taken a day off work, she thought, she might as well take advantage of it to the fullest.

"Sure, I'm game," she said.

Even after spending an exhausting three hours chasing from one department store to another and downing a rushed cup of coffee at the museum, JoJo was reluctant to put a package-laden Barb on the train home.

"I had such a good time," she told Josh's mother honestly as they left her at the outside doors that led to the train platform. "I hope you come back to town soon."

"Maybe after Christmas," Barb said. Then her face brightened. "But I'll see you at Christmas, won't I?"

Unless Peter and I break up before then. "Sure, I guess," JoJo replied.

Barb kissed Josh, gave JoJo a hug, then went to meet her train. They watched her go, both of them a little sad—although JoJo could tell that Josh's sadness was mixed with sudden relief from the usual day-with-a-parent stress.

"I don't know about you, but I could use a cold beer. And a couch." He winced. "My feet are killing me."

"Mine, too," JoJo said.

Josh looked at his watch. "Hey, I have an idea. Let's grab some beer and go home. It's almost five. Peter should be back from work soon."

"That sounds good," JoJo said. Tired as she was, she still had an adrenaline rush from spending the day having fun, and she didn't want to go home to her empty apartment. At least waiting for Peter would ensure their hormones remained on an even keel. "I think I would prefer hot tea over cold beer, though."

"I can probably manage to rustle up some tea for you," Josh assured her.

They took the El home, which was crowded since it was close to rush hour. At the deli near Josh and Peter's apartment, Josh picked up beer and chips to snack on until they worked up the stamina to decide what to do for dinner.

"I haven't been this worn-out in a long time," Josh said as they climbed the steps to his apartment. "I feel like I've just run a marathon."

"I know. I can't believe your mom's energy," JoJo said. "No wonder she's such a rail!"

"I didn't notice you breathing too hard, either," Josh said accusingly. "Whenever I saw you two veer off toward another sale rack, I would go try on more shoes so I could sit down."

JoJo laughed. "I wondered what you were up to."

"Now I also have a backache from leaning over trying on a million different pairs of shoes."

"You're such a whiner!" She went to the kitchen to put hot water on for tea. "I can't believe you tried that many pairs of shoes on without buying any, though. I know I wouldn't have been able to resist."

Josh put his six-pack in the fridge. "Regardless of what you might think, I am able to resist some temptation." She caught his penetrating gaze over the refrigerator door. The tiny kitchen all at once seemed even smaller. "*Some* temptation," he repeated for emphasis.

"Josh . . ."

Suddenly the phone rang, causing them both to jump. Josh shut the refrigerator door and leaned over the counter to pick up the phone. "Hey, bud," he said after hearing who was on the other end, "we were just waiting for you. Yeah, JoJo and I are hanging out here at the apartment."

JoJo looked up at Josh's face, trying to gauge Peter's responses in his expression. She still felt strung tighter than a high wire from his very pointed innuendo. Did he mean that he was still tempted by her?

"How late?" Josh was asking.

JoJo's heart sank. Peter was working late. Again. Why did he do this to her?

"Oh, so you won't be at the office," Josh said, as much to keep her updated as for his own clarification. He listened for a moment, squinting his eyes at what he was hearing. "That's weird, Pete."

JoJo frowned quizzically and Josh shook his head at her. Something strange was going on.

"Okay, whatever you say." Josh looked up. "You want to talk to JoJo?" There was a silence as Peter replied. But JoJo didn't have to hear Peter's voice to be able to tell that his answer was no. A rush of anger burned in her cheeks as she leaned against the counter. "Okay, bud, see you later."

Josh hung up the phone and immediately took note of JoJo's mood swing. "That was Peter," he said gingerly.

"So I heard. What is he up to?" she asked, still mad that Peter hadn't seen fit to tell her himself.

"I'm not sure," Josh said. "He sounded kind of strange, if you want to know the truth. He said he was going shopping."

JoJo's mouth popped open in astonishment. "Peter?"

Josh lifted his shoulders, confused. "Don't ask me."

"What was his excuse for standing us up this afternoon?" JoJo asked. She hated the shrewish way she sounded, giving Josh the third degree like this, but she couldn't help herself.

Josh hesitated. "He didn't say."

JoJo couldn't believe it. "How rude!"

"I didn't ask him about it."

That didn't let him off the hook in JoJo's estimation. "I can't believe Peter was so thoughtless. He's never been this way before."

"It's no big deal," Josh said casually. "It's not as if my mom's never met the guy, you know."

"I know, but what about us? Doesn't he have the responsibility to be nice to us anymore?"

"Hey," Josh said. He came forward and put his hands on her shoulders soothingly. "I'm not offended. But I can understand why you might be."

JoJo felt tears welling in her eyes and tilted her head down so Josh couldn't see them. Maybe she was overreacting, but she couldn't help feeling as if she'd been abandoned. "It's as if I don't exist to Peter anymore," she said.

"Are you two still having problems?" Josh asked.

"More than ever now," JoJo said. "I'm not even sure that Peter really cares for me anymore."

"I can't believe he would take you for granted, Jo," Josh said in a low voice. He put his thumb and forefinger to her chin and tilted her face up to look at him. His eyes were dark with concern. "If that's what he's been doing, he's a fool."

The words were like a balm to JoJo's troubled heart. Why couldn't Peter be this open and affectionate? She put her hands around Josh's neck and looked into his liquid eyes. Did Josh care for her? He must, or he wouldn't be coming on to her this way. Not after what she'd told him, about not being able to settle for an affair. . . .

He'd obviously changed his mind, and now she had to make a choice. Josh or Peter. She felt as though all her affections, loyalties—even her heart itself—were being split in two.

But in the next second, Josh helped her make up her mind. He lowered his head and kissed her coaxingly on the lips. His touch was tentative and sweet and just as wonderful as she remembered it. She sighed and took a step forward into his arms.

"Jo," he said in a husky voice, as though he were trying out what it felt like to say it when they were so wrapped up in each other, so entwined.

She parted her lips and they deepened the kiss, twining their tongues and reveling in the taste of each other. Josh roamed his hands across her shoulders and back, massaging and caressing and soothing the tension there until she felt like modeling clay in his arms. Her body seemed completely warm and fluid, and she touched his own body in a similar fashion, trying to duplicate the effect for him.

He groaned and pulled her closer yet, so that the entire length of their bodies was touching—her soft breasts to his muscled chest, their abdomens and legs—until she felt completely a part of him. Then, without warning, he picked her up.

She moaned softly and rested her head against his chest as he carried her. She had expected him to carry her over to the couch, but instead he hooked a left and moved swiftly toward the bedrooms down the hall.

They passed Peter's room and suddenly JoJo's heart started pounding a mile a minute. They were betraying Peter. But if they loved each other...

Josh strode through the doorway and kicked it lightly closed behind them. In the silence of the strange room, JoJo's heart felt constricted. She looked at the strange bed and her throat tightened.

They did love each other, didn't they? She was no puritan, but the idea of just jumping in and out of some guy's bed didn't appeal to her. She wanted to at least feel secure that the relationship meant something to the person she was attracted to.

"Josh, please," she said. Her voice was a raspy whisper.

Without putting her down, he looked down at her with narrowed dark eyes full of desire. "Is something wrong? If you're worried about protection—"

JoJo shook her head and tried to swallow against the dryness in her throat. "It's not just that," she said. She lifted a hand to touch his cheek. "I need to know where this is all leading."

He stared at her for a moment, uncomprehending, then paled as understanding dawned. Slowly he set her feet down but held on to her arms. "I told you where this is leading, Jo. Nowhere."

Nine

JoJo felt the blood drain from her face. Her legs were rubbery and weak beneath her. "Nowhere?" she repeated, as if she hadn't heard him correctly.

Surely, *surely,* she hadn't heard him correctly. There was no way someone who had kissed her as he had, and looked at her with such searing intensity, could actually believe their chemistry wouldn't be allowed to exist beyond this bedroom. Or had she completely misread the signals?

"I told you that before," Josh said.

"But I thought..." Her words trailed off. His hands slid away from her arms, and she felt suddenly cold. And so, so incredibly foolish. Apparently, no matter how it had seemed to her, she had thought wrong.

"Look," Josh said, his voice an enticing purr, "I think you're sexy. I want to make love to you, Jo. That's not an insult."

His flattery—what bare form of it he was willing to offer her—came too late. "But that's all you want," JoJo assumed aloud.

"All?" Josh took a step forward and she leaned away from him, her arms folded across her chest. "Jo, I think we could have a really incredible physical relationship."

JoJo nearly flinched as it struck her that he was reiterating that *physical* was all a relationship between them would be. "Behind Peter's back?" she asked. "No."

Josh looked at her intently. "I thought, since you were so upset, that maybe you and Peter were breaking up."

"But you knew I hadn't discussed that with him yet," JoJo said. Her mind briefly replayed the events leading up to this crazy moment—the afternoon with Barb, the phone call from Peter, her disappointment. Maybe Josh did actually believe she and Peter were through.

But that just made his sex-only attitude toward her all the more bewildering. He obviously wasn't interested in pursuing a relationship with her, even if they were the last people alive on earth! She felt betrayed, foolish and seethingly angry.

"Look, Jo, even if you and Peter were breaking up, I wouldn't flaunt my relationship with you in front of him. Pete's my friend."

Ire surged through JoJo's veins, and she couldn't bite back a hot retort. "Some friend! You'll steal his girlfriend, but you won't let him know about it. How nice!" She thought with bitter irony of the night she and Josh had made fun of Peter for being Mr. Ethics. That was one trait she wouldn't take for granted again.

"You're hardly in a position to take the moral high ground here. That kiss wasn't one-sided, Jo, and you know it."

She looked up at his unrepentant face and felt another surge of anger at herself. His words were true. What was *her* excuse? "I thought you had changed your mind," she said.

"You should have asked."

"I was under the old-fashioned impression that when two people sleep together, it means something."

"We talked about this," Josh explained. "I'm not into commitment, Jo."

JoJo felt tears gathering again and cursed to herself. She didn't want to start bawling in front of Josh now—that would be too pathetic. Why should she feel like such a dweeb for caring about someone? She *did* care for Josh, too.

Otherwise she would never have let things get so out of hand.

"What *are* you into, Josh?" She wanted to stay calm, to discuss this like an adult, but she couldn't keep the indignation out of her voice. "Is sex all you want?"

"I'm twenty-four," Josh said. "I can't make promises at this stage in my life."

"Twenty-four-year-olds aren't kids anymore, Josh."

"I didn't say I was."

"You're acting like it, though. People grow up when they decide to start making adult choices, not when they reach a certain age."

He smirked. "Thank you, Miss Psychological Development."

JoJo rolled her eyes in frustration, but realized that Josh just might be proving her off-the-cuff theory wrong. Maybe *some* twenty-four-year-olds weren't adults, not in the way she understood the term. And for the first time, she felt relief that she hadn't become involved with Josh before she realized her error.

It would have been a big mistake, she told herself, and the fault would have been hers. Josh wasn't completely to blame.

"We obviously want different things at this point in our lives," she said.

"You say that as if what I want is wrong," Josh said, mirroring her cross-armed stance. "But let me ask you this. Why do you want to throw your life away on one person when you're twenty-three?"

Throw her life away? "Because I want something permanent, someone who'll stick by me...." *Someone not like my father,* she wanted to say. Josh definitely didn't fit that bill.

"But you're young," Josh argued. "You've got your whole life ahead of you to find that someone."

"I want to start my life now," JoJo said, meaning it. "I want marriage, and kids someday. I guess I haven't figured out a way to go about attaining those things yet." Any more than she had figured out how to judge men's characters.

He shrugged. Obviously they would never agree on this point.

"I'd better go home," she said, turning.

Before she could leave, Josh took her arm. When she turned, he was looking into her eyes, his gaze earnest and almost contrite. "I want to be your friend, JoJo, no matter what happens."

"I don't like the reckless way you treat people," she said, her voice low as she remembered his telling Sandy how much he valued her friendship, too. "Especially your friends."

"I mean it," he said. "I've enjoyed hanging out with you. I don't want to lose that."

He just didn't get it. They were on completely different planes, JoJo realized. Josh could be contented with "hanging out," whereas she wanted—no, *needed*—something more substantial.

"I'm sure we'll see each other, Josh," she said. "I just hope it's not too awkward."

She shrugged gently away from him, turned and left the apartment. On the way out she picked up her coat, and she put it on as she was going down the stairs. Not until she hit the cold air outside did she realize that she'd left her hat, coat and scarf upstairs. The scarf that had tied her hair back was also gone, but it didn't matter. Peter could retrieve them for her.

If she ever saw Peter again.

Good Lord, what had she done?

She'd never consciously meant to end things with Peter, but now she was so muddled, she didn't know for sure where they stood. He'd seemed so distant lately. Had she truly just

become carried away with Josh, or were things finished between her and Peter?

How would she ever be able to face him?

All the way back to her little apartment, she tried to sort
out her jumble of feelings. *Josh!* What was the matter with
her? She'd known for years that he was no bedrock of sta-
bility, especially where women were concerned. Peter was
always calling him a bounder, a Casanova. Even if Josh had
wanted a relationship, it probably wouldn't have been long-
lived. He wasn't capable of sustaining a serious commitment. He'd admitted that to her frankly.

He wasn't the kind of guy she was looking for at all. After living with the repercussions of her father's flightiness,
she thought she would have learned that by now. He'd been
a happy-go-lucky type like Josh, too, but once he married
her mother, he had refused to accept the responsibility that
marriage and family meant. And JoJo couldn't help it; she
wanted to be married, and have kids.

But what was she looking for—Peter?

Peter hadn't been quite living up to her dreams, either.
Maybe her standards of compatibility were too unrealistic.

She didn't know what to do. All she knew was that she
needed some time to herself, away from Peter and Josh, to
think things through. To keep going out with Peter without
understanding how she felt about him would be wrong—
both for him and for herself.

On the corner of a busy street not far from her apartment, a Salvation Army Santa was ringing a bell noisily and
cheerfully. The happy sound was completely incongruent
with her mood, but still she took a coin out of her purse and
heard it clang as she dropped it into the donation pot.

"Merry Christmas!" the Santa boomed.

JoJo attempted a smile as she continued on. Christmas—that vacation she was supposed to spend with Peter
and his whole family, because her family was going to be out

of the country. It looked as if it were shaping up to be a dismal holiday. Unless a miracle occurred.

Josh was two beers down by the time Peter made it home an hour and a half later. He couldn't believe he'd blown it so bad with JoJo. He wondered if she'd even talk to him anymore after what had just happened between them.

"Hey, pal," Peter said, shedding his coat and scarf. "Where's Jo? I thought she was over here."

"She was." Josh, who had ensconced himself in his usual chair, didn't look up from the television. He wasn't sure he could face Peter just now—his friend could always read him too well. "She left," he explained simply.

"Good." Peter ran to the kitchen to get himself a beer. He did a little jig around their old couch, as if JoJo's having stomped out an hour and a half earlier was the best news he'd heard in a long time.

Josh pushed himself up to an alert position in his chair. *"Good?"* he asked, his tone unbelieving. Had his friend gone insane? "Pete, I think you'd better call her—"

"I will, I will," Peter said, swatting a hand in eager dismissiveness. "First, I've got to tell you about what I just bought."

He snatched the pad of paper and pen from next to the phone—an apartment rule no-no Peter himself insisted on—and sat on the couch. Placing the pad on the coffee table, he began to sketch with all the ferocity of a kindergarten kid drawing his house for the teacher. His eyes were squinted, and he bit his lower lip in concentration.

He straightened up after a moment, but kept a hand cupped over his masterpiece for a moment as he drew before uncovering it for Josh. "Here, look at what I'm working on and tell me what you think."

Suddenly interested, Josh leaned in closer to inspect what he was doing. "You bought a Hula Hoop?"

"No, no," Peter said, laughing mischievously. "Think smaller." He embellished the circular object on the page as Josh watched in silence. When he was finished, he put down his pencil and grinned in satisfaction. "Isn't it fantastic?"

Josh frowned. "What is it?"

"A ring! What does it look like?"

"A circle with blobs on it."

Peter smiled. "That's what it is, only that big blob is an emerald, and those little clusters of blobs are tiny diamonds."

Josh whistled long and low. "Where is it?"

"At the jeweler's. I'm having it engraved." He waited in silence for Josh to respond further.

Try as he might, Josh couldn't force words past his lips, especially not with Peter watching him eagerly, as though the ring were for him.

"What's the matter?" Peter asked.

Startled, Josh looked up from the paper. "I was just wondering why you decided to run out and buy a ring. I mean, something like this looks...expensive."

"Are you kidding? It was! But this isn't just any old ring. It's an engagement ring." Peter waited for the effect his words were going to have on his friend.

"Engagement!" Josh smiled for all he was worth, though he could hardly contain his shock.

He couldn't believe what a heel he was—and how lucky he was that JoJo had more scruples than he did. To think they had been on the verge of betraying Peter while he was out buying an engagement ring! He felt so ashamed, but there was no way on earth he was going to let Peter know that, not when he seemed so happy, so hopeful.

Josh remembered vividly how angry JoJo had been with Peter, how upset—upset enough nearly to sleep with someone else. Peter would have to do some fancy footwork to win her over again. But how could he convince his friend of that without revealing the depth of his own involvement with JoJo? He didn't want to mess things up more than he already had.

Peter regarded him eagerly during the silence, then added quickly, "I want you to be best man at the wedding. How does that sound?"

"Best man," Josh repeated. He could hardly believe it. Peter was his best friend—of course he would stand up for him. Only, it seemed so strange to think of them already starting to get married. Josh didn't have any brothers or sisters to have preceded him down the aisle, so this was all completely new to him. If Peter got married, this would be the first wedding he attended of one of his peers.

If Peter got married. He might have just screwed that plan up for his best friend. If only he could turn back the clock!

"Aren't you going to congratulate me?" Peter asked nervously.

Josh considered for a moment. "I'm a little surprised, bud. I was with JoJo all afternoon, you know, and she didn't tell me you two were engaged."

"We're not," Peter explained. "Not yet, anyway. I've still got to ask her, but..."

Josh looked at him, and knew by the alarm in Peter's brown eyes that he had registered some of his own skepticism. "Aren't you assuming a lot here?"

"Why?" Peter asked.

Josh shrugged, then darted his gaze back down to the ring and kept it there. He felt like slime. "I don't know. I guess I just feel kind of guilty for seeing the ring before JoJo."

The muscles in Peter's face fell slack. "Is there some kind of rule about that? I mean, I know the groom's not supposed to see the wedding dress." He felt a rush of panic. "This is all new to me. I never heard anything about rings."

"Pete, wait." Josh smiled. "There's no rule about rings. I was just wondering, aren't you putting the cart before the horse here?"

"I want you to be my best man," Peter explained. "So why shouldn't you see—"

"Shouldn't you talk to JoJo first?"

Peter let the question sink in, then sank back on the couch, resting his beer on his knee. "You don't think JoJo will marry me," he said at last.

"I didn't mean—"

"Has she said something to you?"

"Not about that," Josh assured him. "Only…well, where were you today at noon, bud?"

Peter's eyes widened in surprise at the question. "Noon? I was out shopping for this ring. You would have been proud of me—I barely did a lick of work all day."

"I think you forgot something, though. JoJo was trying to call you."

Peter went pale as a sliver of a memory became clear. "Oh, no!" he cried, suddenly realizing his blunder. "Your mom was in town today!"

"Bingo," Josh said.

Peter leapt up and practically hurdled the couch in one bound to get to the phone. "What can I say?"

"You might want to start by apologizing. And then you could follow up by telling her about that expensive ring you bought her," Josh suggested.

Peter held the receiver in his hands nervously. He couldn't believe, after thinking about JoJo all day long, he'd screwed up so royally. It figured he'd decide to be impulsive on the one day it was imperative for him to stick to the schedule!

"I can't tell her about the ring," he said. "It's a surprise."

Josh's eyebrows rose comically. "If not the ring, then don't you at least think you should tell JoJo about the engagement? Otherwise, it's going to be really hard to plan a wedding."

"Ha, ha," Peter said lifelessly. "Of course I'm going to tell her—I mean *ask* her—but not until Christmas."

Josh's expression said doom, which made Peter's stomach roil with nerves. "She's really mad, isn't she?" he asked.

Josh nodded. "She seemed a little miffed."

"Maybe I should go over in person," Peter said.

"I wouldn't do that, either."

"What would you do?"

Josh looked away, pensive for a moment. When he spoke, his voice was soft and thoughtful. "I would apologize," he said sincerely.

"Some help you are—like a broken record! Of course I'm going to apologize. That doesn't always help, though." He looked to Josh for more aid and received none. Abruptly, he set the phone down. "I'm going to see her," he said. It would be good impulsiveness training for him.

He went to his room to change and found himself practically out of clean clothes. Great. All he had were light blue work shirts, which didn't quite suit his mood.

"Hey, pal," he called out. "Mind if I borrow a shirt?"

"Nah, go ahead," Josh said.

Peter trotted down the hall to Josh's room and automatically stooped to pick up a sock from the floor and toss it into the clothes hamper. Only it wasn't a sock, but a scarf. A filmy black scarf he'd seen a thousand times.

He brought it closer to his face, sniffing its light flowery scent. Roses. JoJo sometimes wore perfume that smelled like roses. But why was her scarf on Josh's floor?

Maybe she'd left it a while back, and it had gotten mixed up in their laundry. That happened a lot, since she spent

quite a bit of time over here. Once, one of JoJo's silky ted-
dies had inadvertently landed in their laundry, and then
made its way to Josh's sock drawer. One of Josh's girlfriends found it there and kicked up quite a fuss.

The scarf hadn't been through the laundry, though, and
it had been sitting in a clump all by itself in the middle of the
floor as if JoJo had just dropped it there. Maybe she'd just
left it today. But why would it be in Josh's bedroom?

Peter didn't want to think the horrible thought that came
into his head. He was not a suspicious person by nature.
And there weren't two people on earth he trusted more than
Josh and JoJo.

So why was a terrible knot of anxiety forming in the pit
of his stomach?

His shirt dilemma completely forgotten, he stomped out
of the room, shoving the scarf into his pocket. "I think I'll
give her a call after all," he said as he came back out into the
living room. "She might not want company after a long day
of running around the city."

"That's a good idea," Josh said. He hadn't moved from
the couch.

Peter dialed the number, feeling as though he had just lost
his best friend. His *two* best friends. The faint hope that
JoJo would sound perky and glad to hear from him was
dashed immediately. Her voice was strained when she said
hello.

"Hi, it's me," Peter said. "I'm calling to grovel and
apologize and beg your forgiveness."

His words brought a nervous laugh from the other end of
the line. "Why?"

"Why? Only because I forgot all about lunch, that's
why!" Peter said, astonished that she had to ask. "I'm so
sorry, Jo. Josh told me you'd been trying to call."

"Oh, that. It's no big deal," JoJo said. She didn't sound at all angry, as Josh had warned. But the disparity in their stories only served to make him more suspicious.

"I'll make it up to you, I promise. How about dinner, or we could—"

"Can it be some other time?" JoJo asked, breaking in. "I'm really tired. Plus I need to work on my monologue for that class next Monday."

Peter felt the disappointment down to the marrow of his bones. "Sure," he said.

"I guess I overdid today," JoJo explained. "Barb's so full of energy."

"I understand," Peter said. It was just as he'd expected, he told himself. She was tired after a long day of running around the city. So why didn't he feel reassured?

"Good night, then," he said. "I love you."

"I'll talk to you soon," JoJo replied.

Peter hung up the phone with a heavy heart. She hadn't said "I love you, too," or anything that would have put his mind at ease. In fact, her voice had sounded heavy when she'd mentioned talking to him soon, as if she had something horrible to discuss.

But if she wasn't mad at him for missing lunch today, what was she upset about?

As if by instinct, his hand slipped into his pocket and felt the silky material there. His glance darted to Josh, who was studiously watching a rerun of an old sitcom on the television, avoiding looking at him. Peter felt a terrible lurch in the pit of his stomach as his suspicions grew all out of proportion in his mind.

He had to get out of the apartment.

"I think I'll go down to Razzles," he told Josh. "Wanna come?"

Josh shook his head slowly from side to side. "No, thanks."

As he left the apartment building, Peter was glad Josh hadn't wanted to accompany him. Otherwise he couldn't have been sure he wouldn't have attacked his friend and tried to shake the truth out of him about that scarf.

Ten

JoJo sat in a folding chair in the corner of a tiny rehearsal room and watched three actors performing a scene from Chekhov's *The Seagull*. She'd always thought the play was depressing, but tonight it seemed fascinating, especially the way Otto Kleist worked with the actors to get more emotional impact from them.

And somehow, the story of a young actress's melodramatic descent into despair never seemed quite so relevant to her own life as it did tonight. Not that she was anywhere near as desperate as Nina—the young actress in the drama taking shape on stage—but she'd never felt herself at such a crossroads before in her life, either. And seeing what happened when someone made a wrong turn made her realize the importance of making the right one.

She hadn't spoken to Peter for nearly a week. He'd left several messages on her answering machine, but she'd been screening her calls. She just didn't know what to tell him. Airing the truth might irreversibly rupture his friendship with Josh—and rupture their own relationship, as well. What purpose would that serve?

But to keep the truth from him, and continue to date him while she had questions about where it was all leading, was equally unfeasible to her. She didn't want to use Peter, holding on to him just in case something better didn't come along. She would feel terrible if some man did that to her.

Yet avoiding Peter wasn't solving anything, either; sooner or later, they would have to talk. But if it was too soon, she worried that he would be able to read her thoughts, to see right through her to the terrible truth. Though she and Josh hadn't actually had sex, she felt as if they'd betrayed Peter in a terrible way all the same.

In fact, she often wondered what would have happened if Josh hadn't been truthful with her. Would she have slept with him and regretted it later, or would she have eventually fallen into his own casual attitude toward male-female relationships as a way of rationalizing her own behavior? She'd seen lots of girls pretending not to care that their boyfriends didn't treat them well, just so they themselves wouldn't look foolish for caring too much. At least she hadn't been caught in that trap, JoJo thought.

But she didn't want to use Peter as a consolation prize. After two years, she owed him more than that. Unfortunately, she owed him more than the silent treatment she'd been giving him lately, too.

"Are you walking to the El?"

JoJo looked over at the person sitting next to her, a woman in her late twenties named Marnie. She was tall and waiflike, with pale blue eyes and strawberry blond hair. In contrast to her paleness, however, the actress was dressed entirely in black, right down to her clunky combat boots. They had talked during the break and discovered they lived not too far away from each other.

"Sure," JoJo said. She ran over to tell Otto how much she enjoyed his class and looked forward to working on a scene. She had done one of her monologues tonight, and he had given her pointers to jazz it up for her to practice. She would perform it again when the class next met after Christmas.

"Say hello to Barb for me," Otto said in his boisterous voice, then winked. "Tell her I'm as fit and trim as ever."

JoJo laughed along with him. Otto weighed three hundred if he weighed a pound. She didn't want to laugh too much, though, since she'd just met the man. And as she walked away with Marnie, she thought he looked rather sad, left alone in the little rented studio space, pushing the chairs back against the wall.

"Does Otto have family here in Chicago?" she asked Marnie as they made their way down the sidewalk on the cold evening.

Marnie scrunched up her shoulders. "I don't know. I'm sure he has friends, though."

JoJo nodded. She had had a sudden flash of Otto alone on Christmas, for all his looking a little like Santa Claus. But maybe she should be worrying about her own Christmas status, given that she was still on the rocks with Peter.

"What about you?" Marnie asked. "Do you have family here?"

"Yes, my mother and her second husband."

Marnie nodded. "Lucky."

"I hardly ever see them. My mother works in sales, so she travels a lot." She frowned. "Do you mean you don't have family here?"

Marnie shook her head. "No. I came here from Omaha after college, without knowing anybody really, hoping for a break. That was six years ago. Guess maybe it wasn't a wise move."

JoJo shivered, and not entirely from the cold. She gathered her coat around her, glad she wasn't so alone herself. As she glanced to the side, Marnie's pale complexion and cornflower-blue eyes seemed wan and forlorn. "But you're going home for Christmas, aren't you?" she asked. "To Omaha?"

"If I can scrape together enough money," Marnie said. "One year I didn't have enough for even a bus ticket. That was a bummer."

She couldn't even afford a bus ticket to Omaha? How depressing! The poor woman needed to find a better line of work. "What do you do? For money, I mean," JoJo asked Marnie.

"I'm a temp."

"Oh."

"I've temped since coming to Chicago. It keeps my schedule open for auditions." She ducked her head self-consciously. "Not that I've had much luck, but there's always the hope."

"Mmm." JoJo's heart felt as though it weighed a million pounds. "I've done a lot of temping, too."

"Then you understand what I'm talking about. Usually I get plenty of work, but every once in a while you hit a dry patch."

JoJo had hit more than her share of dry patches. Just last month it had taken her over a week to get assigned and she had been painfully short of cash—so Peter had treated her to dinners out. And then there were plenty of other instances when she'd mooched off him at his apartment. Once, when she was really strapped, she'd gotten a loan off him to make sure her electricity didn't get cut off.

Whenever she hit rock bottom, Peter had been there, to take her out to the movies or to a ball game. She'd never been without a support network. And she'd never been alone on Christmas.

"I guess it is a pretty fly-by-night way to live," she admitted.

"It's the only way!" Marnie said with a fervent gleam in her eye. "An actress has to keep her schedule open."

Even at the expense—literally—of going home at Christmas, or paying the phone bill? Suddenly the very idea seemed kind of crazy to JoJo; she wondered how Peter—Mr. Practical—could have let her go this long without drumming some sense into her brain. And she'd only been out of school for two years—Marnie was twenty-eight!

"It must be nice to have family in town," Marnie said wistfully. "Do you have a boyfriend, too?"

"Yes," she answered, then amended, "sort of. Do you?"

Marnie shook her head. "I did, but we broke up. He wanted to get married and move to *Iowa!*"

"My boyfriend went to college in Iowa," JoJo said. "He loved it there."

Marnie rolled her eyes. "I know it's probably a perfectly good state and everything, but what would *I* have done there? Can you imagine what the theater situation must be like in Sioux City?"

JoJo laughed along with Marnie halfheartedly. "So... what did you tell your boyfriend?"

"I told him it was me or Iowa." In the silence that followed it was apparent which the guy had opted for. Marnie shrugged. "No big loss. I couldn't live without my career."

What career?

Peter's stark, harsh words, the ones he had hurled at her on the car ride home from Wisconsin, reverberated through JoJo's mind, but remained unspoken. She wasn't close enough to Marnie to say them to her, but she was suddenly grateful to Peter for having the nerve to take her to task for not looking at life realistically. She had wondered several times how Barb could have traded a life in soap operas for Wisconsin. Now she knew.

Barb had probably run into a few Marnies too many. Seeing an actress with no family, no money and no acting job was enough to panic anybody. It certainly panicked JoJo.

As their train rattled down the tracks, JoJo reappraised Marnie's appearance; it struck her that the waif look in Marnie's case might be a little too authentic. Even though they had just met, she couldn't stand to see someone go hungry.

"Would you like to get a bite to eat?" JoJo asked as they neared their stop. "There's a diner around the corner—the food's greasy, but good."

Marnie looked down at her large fringed bag that served as a purse, as though she could actually see through the leather and tell how much money was inside it. After a moment of contemplation, she shook her head. "I'd better not. I've got pasta at home."

JoJo nodded. "It was just a thought."

The train stopped at their station and they got off. Once on the street, though, they went in different directions.

"I'll see you after Christmas," JoJo said as they stopped to exchange phone numbers. "I hope you make it to Omaha this year."

"I'll give you a call," Marnie said. "But if I don't talk to you, Merry Christmas."

JoJo returned the words and watched for a moment as Marnie headed in the opposite direction. Somehow, the sight of her thin body retreating in the now-drizzly cold night saddened her. She looked—*was*—so alone.

She turned and started back for her own apartment. One thing was certain—she wanted to be more together than Marnie was when she was twenty-eight. By that time, she wanted to have a stable career, and be married, maybe even with a kid.

In short, all she wanted was a normal life. Millions of people managed to have one...so why was it something she had so much trouble with?

JoJo moped over the question for the rest of the long week, remaining indecisive about what to do about Peter. Then she got a call she felt sure would change her life.

She put the phone down carefully, so shocked she could hardly believe it. She had a job! An acting job—sort of! For the first time in her life, she was actually going to be paid to do something other than answering phones, typing letters or scooping French fries into little paper bags.

She stood for a moment, looking at her cramped apartment, with the futon that served as a bed and a couch, and the little coffee table that she banged her knee on every morning, and her bookcase overflowing with books and scripts. It was the same marginal apartment she'd been living in for two years, only now she felt . . . successful!

An energetic whoop worked its way up her throat and came out of her mouth loud and strong. She jumped in the air, doing one of those crazy leaps cheerleaders used to perform in high school but she had never learned how to do. That's what she felt like—her own cheerleading squad. *Give me a J!* she thought happily, then caught herself. She was so happy she was losing her mind.

Okay, the job was only a voice-over for a shoe store. Calm down, she told herself. It was no big deal. Act cool.

She walked across the room to get a diet soda out of her fridge, practicing being composed while her heart was palpitating, her feet felt like dancing and her mind was prematurely composing her Oscar acceptance speech. She couldn't help it. She popped open her fizzy drink and giggled like a half-wit.

She had to tell people! She had to tell the *world!*

First, her mom. She leapt for the phone and dialed the number quickly. The phone rang and rang, and then the answering machine picked up. At the sound of the beep, JoJo took a deep breath to speak, then hung up the phone. What was she supposed to say? *Great news, Mom, I got a shoe commercial voice-over!*

Of course, her mom *would* think it was great news. No one had been more supportive of her than her mother, ever since JoJo had played Martha Washington in a school play in third grade. That wasn't really the problem.

The problem was, this was news she wanted to share with someone in person. She immediately thought of Peter. He would explode with happiness when she told him, and insist on celebrating. That's what she wanted. Someone to share with, to celebrate with.

She dialed the number but hung up after one ring. She wanted to see the look on his face when she told him, and for that, she would have to surprise him. Besides, they hadn't talked in a week and a half, so she could at least make the twenty-minute walk to tell him in person. This would give her the perfect excuse to have a reconciliation with him.

She threw a coat over her crinkle skirt, floppy sweater and leggings and headed out the door at a clip. It was fitting that she should tell Peter her good news first—he had been the one to give her that extra shove, after all. He was the one who had forced her to bite the bullet and try. She owed him.

All the way through the darkening streets, she practiced her speech to Peter. *You were right,* she would tell him. *I just needed to get my head on straight. I needed someone to point me in the right direction.*

I needed you, she thought.

She was so lucky to have a friend like him. As mad as he had made her, he'd shaken her out of her rut and gotten her on the move again. After talking to Marnie, she knew how important it was to have someone outside the profession to put things in perspective for you. Poor Marnie was alone, by choice, going at her profession like a gerbil on a wire wheel—and making about as much progress, too.

Outside Peter's building, she buzzed their apartment number and waited impatiently in front of the intercom. Finally Josh's voice came on.

"Hey, Josh, it's me," she said breathlessly. "Can I come up?"

"Uh, sure." But his voice sounded anything but certain. JoJo frowned as a buzz sounded, and the lock on the outside glass door was released with a click.

She shook off a brief sense of foreboding and took the stairs two at a time. Once she reached the apartment, she was breathless and giddy again, ready to spill her news. Josh opened the door before she could knock, and she swept inside.

"I've got the greatest news!" she cried, unbuttoning her coat. "Where's Peter?" JoJo looked down the hallway toward the bedrooms, expecting to see his blond head dart out to see her.

Josh, still standing by the door in his jeans and an unbuttoned shirt, crossed his arms. "I thought he had told you. He went home."

JoJo paled. "Home? Is anything wrong?"

"No, no, just the opposite. His sister-in-law had her baby so he buzzed up for the weekend to get a look at his new niece."

"Oh... A niece, that's terrific."

Josh tapped his bare toes on the wood floors and shifted feet. "They named her Jennifer."

"Pretty name." Disappointment stabbed at her insides, along with a twinge of hurt. She couldn't believe Peter hadn't called her. When his other niece was born, they had all gone out on the spur of the moment to Razzles to celebrate. A thought occurred to her. "So was she born today? I guess she must have if Peter went running off...."

Josh shook his head. "No, the baby was born two days ago. I can't believe he didn't tell you...."

JoJo frowned, then shrugged lightly, as if it were no big deal that Peter was no longer telling her the momentous things that happened in his life. "Oh, well. I guess he's been busy with his new job and all."

Josh sniffed and nodded quickly. "Yeah. I haven't seen much of him, either. He hasn't been around the apartment much, to tell the truth. Not since—" His mouth snapped shut abruptly. But he didn't have to finish. JoJo knew exactly what he was talking about.

Her eyes flew open wide. "You didn't tell him anything that would make him suspicious, did you?"

"No, of course not," Josh said, lowering his voice as though Peter could hear them all the way from Wisconsin. "But why have you been giving him the cold shoulder? I know he's called you." There was a hint of reproach in his voice.

She frowned and felt her shoulders sag a little. "I just needed some time to think. Things seemed so crazy...."

Josh nodded. "Yeah."

There was a pause, then suddenly the air seemed tense and awkward. The apartment was too quiet, too still. It was Friday night; why didn't Josh have the stereo playing or the TV on? He was staring at a point behind JoJo's shoulder and she whipped around to see what had drawn his eye.

When she saw the object of his gaze, JoJo felt herself go pale with shock, then red with embarrassment.

A redhead. The beautiful willowy woman with long russet hair atumble was wrapped in a man's bathrobe, her long legs bare to her bright fire-engine-red painted toes. Her wide pouty mouth smiled coyly at JoJo in greeting. "Hey," she said in a high whispery voice.

The corners of JoJo's mouth curled up tightly. "Hi," she said in return. She turned back around and shot Josh a look of pure disbelief. "You didn't tell me you had company."

Josh shrugged. "I didn't know you were going to pop in for a visit. This is Chloe." He pointed to the woman, as if JoJo couldn't guess whom he was referring to.

"Hello," JoJo said politely. It wasn't the woman's fault that she had been taken in by a schmuck.

Suddenly a wave of disgust rushed through her. She couldn't even work up an ounce of jealousy for the red-head, or anger at Josh for having rebounded so success-fully from their aborted romance. All she could think about was what a dope she was—how had she let herself be taken in by Josh, the world's biggest smoothy?

She started rebuttoning her coat. "I just came by to see Peter," she clarified, in case he was suffering any delusions that she had "popped in" to see him. "When will he be back?" she asked.

"Sunday night."

"Fine." JoJo moved past Josh, who stopped her before she could reach the door by clamping a hand around her forearm. She threw him a resentful, questioning look.

"What was your good news?" he asked.

"I was going to tell Peter that I got a job in a commercial."

"That's terrific, JoJo," Josh said.

"Wow!" Chloe exclaimed from the hallway. "A commercial."

Josh grimaced. "Chloe wants to get into acting, too." Then, brightening, he gave JoJo's arm a little punch. "Hey, that's great! Didn't I tell you it would all work out? You deserve it."

JoJo rolled her eyes. All she felt she deserved right now was a big kick in the pants. She was such an idiot! "Will you tell Peter to call me when he comes in on Sunday?"

"Sure," Josh said. "Don't you want to stick around for a minute, to celebrate?"

Some celebration that would be, she thought. *Me, Josh and his latest squeeze.* "I don't think so," she said. "Have a nice weekend."

She turned and fled down the stairs, glad to get away from Josh and his new object of desire. She couldn't believe it! All those weeks she'd been taking him seriously, as though he had actually cared for her, or might. She felt ashamed for getting so carried away.

Had she really considered calling it quits with Peter over Josh? She couldn't believe it. And now Peter wasn't talking to her.

Maybe Josh was right. Maybe she had finally gotten what she deserved.

Just because she and Peter had hit a snag, she had thrown away the best relationship in her life. And for what? For the first man who had smiled at her! And now, a week later, that man was cozied up with a redhead, and she was alone in Chicago on a Friday night, on what should have been one of the happiest nights of her life.

This was the beginning of her life as a professional actress, and already she felt like one of those pathetic women Susan Lucci might play in a miniseries about how lonely it is at the top. It was almost laughable.

It would be, if she didn't miss Peter so much. All week she had been afraid that she would just be turning to him because he was convenient, the guy she'd been going out with forever. She'd lost sight of the fact that she felt closer to him than any other person on the planet. He really was her Rock of Gibraltar; without him her world felt tilted, off-balance. Would it ever be set right again?

Eleven

"**I**'m so proud of you!" JoJo's mother said. She was especially proud when JoJo told her the generous sum the shoe company would be paying her to use her voice in their commercial. "What a nice Christmas present for you."

"Yeah." JoJo's reply came out less than enthusiastic, and she winced as she felt her mother tune into her unhappiness over the wire.

"Are you okay, honey?"

"I'm fine, Mom. I'm just not looking forward to Christmas so much this year."

"You're still going to Peter's, aren't you?" She sounded worried.

But not as worried as JoJo felt inside. With her mother and stepfather going to Europe this week, it was possible she might very well end up alone for Christmas.

"Yeah, I think so," she said just to make her mother—and maybe herself—feel better.

"JoJo..."

JoJo sighed. "Okay, maybe not. Peter and I are kind of like going through a tough time right now."

"'Kind of like'? What does that mean?"

Her mother always corrected the ticks in her speech, regardless of how dire the situation was. "We *are* going through a tough time."

After much tongue-clicking and *hmm*ing on the other end of the line, her mother shifted into problem-solving maternal gear. "It's too late to get you on a plane to Germany, I'm afraid. I suppose you could visit your father. Do you need to borrow some money?''

"That's okay, Mom. I'm sure I'll be going to Wisconsin," she lied. "Besides, I don't know if I could take Dad just now."

That much was the truth. After her fiasco with Josh, she wasn't sure she could be around her father, especially during the holidays. He never even had a tree, or fixed Christmas dinner.

"I worry about you being alone," her mother said.

Something Barb had said came back to JoJo suddenly, something she hadn't given much credence at the time. Barb had told her not to get so involved in her career that her personal life suffered for it. Is that what she had done, without realizing it? Maybe Josh had only been part of the problem. She hadn't felt she needed Peter, because she had other things in life she was working on. How could she have been so stupid?

Maybe because she had never felt this alone before.

She'd certainly hadn't felt this alone the night she had her first audition and Peter had shown up at her door with dinner. She'd practically blown him off then. And the time he'd surprised her after his promotion, all she'd been able to think about was Josh, and how Peter only wanted to celebrate because of his job. All the times he'd tried to be nice to her, she'd rebuffed him or soft-pedaled his affection for her for her own selfish reasons.

For her mother's sake, she forced her voice to remain steady and calm. "Don't worry, I'll have the guys. Peter and Josh won't let me starve on Christmas."

She pictured her mother's fretful face. "If you think it's okay...."

"Be sure to tell David Merry Christmas for me," JoJo said. "I miss him bunches."

"I'll call you from the airport," her mother promised.

"Love you," JoJo said.

To her surprise, there were tears spilling down her cheeks. It was Sunday night, well after the time Peter usually tried to get into town after a weekend trip, and he hadn't called. He probably wouldn't, either. She'd blown it.

She considered going to the guys' apartment and begging forgiveness. Maybe she would even tell Peter the truth—he always said it was better to know the truth, no matter how painful, and now she was beginning to see why. By putting Peter off and trying to mull things over on her own, she felt as though she might have actually made things worse. What if she just told him that she'd had a little flirtation? That's all it had been. Nothing had happened, after all.

Nothing except that she'd almost slept with Peter's very best friend in the whole wide world.

But she hadn't gone through with it, she reminded herself. Didn't that count for something? Didn't that mean that maybe she wasn't completely a lost cause as a girlfriend? She wondered whether Peter would see it that way, but she figured she owed it to him to give him the chance to understand, and to try to forgive.

She was going to have to tell him the truth. That was all there was to it. How else could she live with herself?

The phone rang again. With her heart in her throat, JoJo picked it up.

"Hi!"

It was Marnie. JoJo collapsed against the futon in disappointment. "Oh, hi," she returned.

"Gee, glad to talk to you, too," Marnie said sulkily.

"I'm sorry, it's just—"

"Just you were expecting someone male." Marnie laughed. "Same old story. So Peter hasn't called you?"

She and Marnie had gone out to lunch on Saturday, and JoJo had spilled her guts to her new friend about her love life. Now she felt a little foolish. "He might not have gotten back from Wisconsin yet," she rationalized.

"Well, you shouldn't sit around brooding," Marnie said. "The best thing to do is to get out, and concentrate on what really matters."

JoJo frowned and concentrated on twirling the phone cord around her finger. "What's that?"

"Your acting, what else?"

What else was left, was more like it.

When JoJo didn't answer, Marnie continued, "To that end, I think you should come out with me. There's an improv group..."

On and on Marnie expounded about the fabulous improvisational group she'd found at a comedy club nearby, and how it was a wonderful learning experience just to watch them. JoJo wasn't much in the mood for a night of comedy, however. "Oh...I don't know," she said indecisively.

"JoJo, you can't sit inside your apartment forever, waiting for Peter to show up. Where's your backbone?"

Resting lazily against my futon, JoJo thought with a sigh. She didn't want to turn into a complete mope. It was perfectly obvious Peter wasn't going to show up. But should she set out in search of him, confess and watch him blow up, or should she search for a way to forget him?

Tomorrow the ring was going to be ready. Peter had plans for that ring, if only JoJo would cooperate.

It had helped to go home and see the new baby, and his brother, now a proud father twice over. Everyone had been surprised that Peter hadn't brought JoJo with him. His brother cornered him and asked what was wrong between him and JoJo, and after only a little encouragement, Ben had brimmed over with advice. *Be tenacious, she'll come around. Treat her like a princess. If all else fails, get down on your knees and grovel.* Peter smiled, remembering that last bit.

It was almost six on Sunday night, and Peter was determined to end the weekend on a better note than it had begun. His lonely trip up to Wisconsin had been sheer hell, with a million doubts and suspicions running through his mind the entire time. But he was giving JoJo the space she seemed to want, in hopes that she might be glad to see him when he got back.

Of course, the fact that he had left Josh and JoJo alone in the same city for an entire weekend had also preyed on his mind the whole time. He hadn't dared tell Ben his suspicions about his best friend—he knew very well what his brother would have said to him about leaving the two together. *Dumb move, bro. Really dumb.*

He'd told himself he was doing it as a sort of test. He had no evidence to substantiate his suspicions, after all. And if JoJo and Josh had a thing for each other, wouldn't it be better to let it surface so he would at least know the truth? Definitely, he'd thought... before he was a hundred miles away and helpless to do anything to stop whatever it was from surfacing.

The whole trip back he'd been sick with nerves. His best friend and his girlfriend. He couldn't believe it. JoJo and he had watched a movie once called *Betrayal,* one of those boring foreign ones she liked so well, about a man who had an affair with his best friend's wife. Only, the story was told backward, from the end of the affair to the beginning, so that while watching it you wanted to leap onto the screen and stop the actions you knew were inevitably going to happen.

That's how Peter had felt, driving back from Wisconsin. He wanted to warn JoJo, to wave his arms and send up flares telling her that *he* was the right guy for her and that getting involved with Josh would bring her only grief, but knew it was impossible. If she wanted Josh, what could he do? Hormones were stronger than rational explanation. Maybe, sometimes, hormones were stronger than love....

Of course, that didn't mean he couldn't slug Josh anyway, just to make himself feel better.

As he had opened the door to his apartment, he had half expected to see JoJo and Josh in a clench on the couch. Instead, what he witnessed had brought relief to his heart and tears of joy to his eyes. Josh, his wonderful couch-potato friend, was on the couch, all right—but his arm was around a drop-dead gorgeous redhead!

Peter had changed clothes, washed, shaved and run out of the apartment door, feeling as if he'd just been given a new lease on life. He had, he was sure of it. Of course, Josh's taking up with a redhead didn't solve all of Peter's problems with JoJo—but whatever those problems were, they seemed a whole lot more workable than they had this weekend.

He sprinted the entire way to JoJo's apartment, thanking his lucky stars with each footfall on the pavement. It was nice to believe that he would have been a good sport had JoJo and Josh decided that they were in love, but he was just as happy never to have to find out whether that was true!

A man was walking into JoJo's building, and Peter followed him inside, dashing up the three flights to her door. He pounded hastily, and within seconds, the door flew open.

She was standing there with the phone to her ear and wearing a long-sleeved baby-doll shirt, leggings and a big pair of Mickey Mouse slippers. Peter smiled, and she beamed back at him, grabbed his arm with her free hand and pulled him inside. His heart did a little flip-flop in his chest.

"Marnie, I've gotta go," JoJo said into the phone. "Bye!" She dropped the phone back into its cradle, never taking her eyes off him. "Hi."

Suddenly uncomfortable, Peter broke the gaze, then glanced around the little room, looking for clues as to what JoJo had been doing with herself. What he saw made him feel inordinately pleased. There were no telltale ties or boxer shorts in evidence—just scripts.

"I came by to congratulate you," he said with more composure than he felt. "Josh told me about the commercial."

"*I* should congratulate *you*," JoJo said. "You're an uncle again." Then she frowned. "Thanks for telling me, by the way. I had to find out from Josh."

"It didn't seem to me a few weeks ago that you minded talking to Josh."

JoJo's eyes opened wide in alarm at his tone. She turned, marched across the room, placed the phone on the coffee table and sat down on the futon with her hands clasped in front of her. She opened her mouth to speak, then shut it again.

Peter felt awkward. All the big feelings he'd had on the way over were bottlenecked inside his chest, squeezing off the words he'd wanted so much to say to her, all the apologies and promises and declarations. He looked at her hoping for a lead, but she seemed as tongue-tied as he was.

"Oh, hell, JoJo, I don't want to argue."

"I don't, either, Peter," she said, "but maybe—"

Suddenly he crossed the space between them and sat down next to her. "No, don't. Don't say anything about us maybe going through a phase or anything else. That's not why I came over here."

She looked at him anxiously. "Then why are you here?"

"To make a new start."

A light shone in her eyes, but her expression remained doubtful. "Start over...how?"

"A date."

A skeptical smile touched her lips. "A date? As in, you'll pencil me in whenever you have the time?"

"No!" Frustrated, Peter combed a hand through his hair. "I want to take you out right now. Let's go."

He tugged her off the futon but she balked, and stood limp as a wet rag before him. "Right this minute?"

He nodded.

"But we'll miss 'Sixty Minutes,'" JoJo said.

"Forget 'Sixty Minutes,'" he said. "I had a revelation a while back, before things got so weird. I decided I want to spend my life doing spontaneous things with you."

JoJo's face lost some of its tension and she shimmied forward, smiling. "That sounds interesting. What kind of things?" She snaked her arms around his middle.

"Well..." Peter took a deep breath. Her hands felt wonderful. It was all he could do not to throw her down on the futon and reciprocate the gesture. "I thought we could go to a movie."

Her hands stopped. She looked into his eyes, disbelief on her face. "A movie? On a Sunday night?"

"Not just any old movie," Peter said.

JoJo dropped her arms. "I hadn't heard. Does Arnold or Sylvester or Jean-Claude have a new offering for us?"

"You don't like any of those people," Peter said.

"But you do," JoJo answered.

"And you're willing to sit through yet another shoot-'em-up action-adventure thriller just for me?"

She nodded. "Of course."

"Why?"

She bit her lip, then looked at him squarely. Her eyes were moist. "Because I missed you, Peter. I really did. This has been the longest weekend of my life! Right now I'd go see mud wrestling, if that would make you happy."

Peter laughed and gathered her in his arms as his heart rate soared. "It wouldn't," he said. "Actually, I thought we could drop by the Music Box and see one of those foreign things."

She let out a short, sharp bark. "You've got to be kidding!"

"No. I've come to realize that those boring movies can have real resonance in a person's life."

She looked at him with even more doubt. "I think something serious must have happened to you, Peter. Did something bonk you on the head or something?"

That's what it felt like. He felt dizzy with love for her. "I'd sit through a thousand Gérard Depardieu films if that would make you happy, Jo."

She shook her head of shimmering black curls. "Watch it. I might hold you to that."

He gathered her closer and placed a kiss on her lips, reveling in the feeling of her hands lacing behind his neck. This was all he wanted, all he needed, for the rest of his life. He didn't care what differences there were between them, as long as she agreed with him about that.

"Peter..." She pulled her head back and snuggled against his chest, sighing softly.

"What?"

"We don't *have* to go see a movie, do we? I mean, since you want to see Gérard and I want to see Arnold, don't you think we should find something else spontaneous to do as a compromise?"

"I think that would be a really good idea." He lifted her into his arms and they fell in a tumble onto the futon.

"Van Morrison! This is great!"

Peter bumped up "Brown-Eyed Girl" to the car stereo's

most earsplitting level and reached across the gearshift to hold JoJo's hand, as if they were teenagers. In the back seat, Josh smiled at them, a good-natured but uncomfortable fifth wheel. The day was gray and slushy, and traffic was moving slowly, yet inside the car Peter had been bopping to this oldies station ever since they left Chicago, oblivious to the subtle tension in the air.

JoJo felt it. Josh could tell by the way she tugged to retrieve her hand for a few moments, then gave up with a hapless grin.

Josh also knew the reason Peter was so wound up. Somewhere in this car, probably in Peter's suitcase, there was a ring hidden with JoJo's name on it. Peter had been like a kid all week, talking about how he was going to surprise her with a Christmas proposal. But whenever Josh asked when and where it was going to happen—surely, he wouldn't ask her during Christmas dinner or anything like that—his friend would clam up. Josh would just have to wait and see like everybody else, was all he would say.

Josh feared Peter was going to pop the question publicly, which was a situation that frightened him more than it did Peter. In fact, the dangers of doing this never seemed to occur to Peter, but Josh didn't feel he was in a position to tell his friend how risky a venture this could be. He only hoped that JoJo said yes—yet, given her wavering feelings of a week ago, would she? Could she?

Maybe JoJo was the one he should warn. But he couldn't do that, either. There was a possibility that everything would work out fine, and besides, if Peter ever found out that he'd told JoJo, he would lose his best friend, and probably JoJo wouldn't appreciate it, either. She was a big girl and used to thinking fast on her feet. One chunky emerald probably wouldn't intimidate her from speaking her mind, no matter who was looking on.

And there had to be some rationale behind all Peter's manic optimism. Maybe things weren't at all as dire as Josh thought they were. Peter seemed to think everything was fine between JoJo and himself, that whatever glitch had occurred between them had been smoothed over.

Just then, JoJo glanced back at him. "Are you okay back there, Josh? You need more heat?" she yelled over the radio. Not that the overworked heater would crank out much more....

He shook his head. He was wrapped in a coat, hat and muffler. So was JoJo. Only Peter was unbundled—but he'd probably generated too much heat from all that dancing he'd been doing to notice that his car was a little on the frigid side.

She smiled at him, tentatively. They'd hardly spoken since last Friday night, when she'd come over and found Chloe in the apartment. She'd looked upset that night, though Josh couldn't figure that one out at all. *She* had been the one to grind things to a screeching halt between them—wisely, he realized now. He'd told her that he wasn't the committing type.

Not that he didn't want to be. Seeing Peter's happiness these past few days had given him cause for reflection on the subject. Marriage was definitely something he wanted in his future—someday, maybe, say, in about fifteen years.

He just hoped their flirtation hadn't made JoJo so confused that she wouldn't know what to say when Peter did ask her to marry him. In fact, if she said no, Josh was certain he would feel guilty for the rest of his life.

Suddenly Peter turned down the radio. "Hey, pal, you think I should do it now?"

Josh freaked. *"Now?"* he said, his frozen vocal cords creating a loud squeak.

JoJo looked anxiously from one to the other. "Do what?"

Surely Peter wasn't crazy enough to try proposing now, in an ice-cold Volkswagen, with his best friend in the back seat! Josh squirmed with discomfort at what he was about to witness. Sure, he and Peter were best friends and all and had known each other forever, and he appreciated being included, but still. Some things went beyond the call of budship! Why couldn't Peter take JoJo to an expensive restaurant, or a quiet park, and pop the question there? This was so awful.

He looked up at Peter's smiling face in the rearview mirror. "It's your life," he warned his friend ominously.

Then a terrible thought occurred to him. What if Peter had found out about him and JoJo, and this was some kind of retribution? Maybe all that manic energy he'd witness had been just that—mania! Like in those horror movies, where the thwarted boyfriend waited until just the perfect moment to take his revenge. Slick Road Spells Doom for Love Triangle! the headlines could read.

Of course that was ridiculous.... Josh glanced out the window at the fine sheen of oil and icy rain on the highway and felt a shiver go down his spine. "I don't think I should be seeing this, bud," he said.

"Why? You've seen it before," Peter argued.

Josh shook his head, confused. "I have?"

"Sure, remember? You always said I would have a true test of a woman's affection if she could hear me out and still say she loved me afterward."

Josh's memory whirred on high speed, trying like hell to think of some time they'd had a conversation along these lines. But the words about love sounded so hokey, he just couldn't imagine them coming out of his mouth. He shrugged helplessly at both JoJo and Peter. "Sorry, I don't remember."

"Then I guess I'll just have to go ahead without your okay," Peter said.

Oh, no—please don't! Josh thought. He felt clammy and nervous for his friend. Never, ever, would he again put himself in this horrible position, he vowed, getting too involved with a friend and his girlfriend. It was too much guilt, too much stress. Best man. He would be best man—if they ever managed to come through this—but that was it.

Peter cleared his throat, and Josh closed his eyes, waiting for the fateful proposal to come out of his mouth, or a terrible accusation, or for the car to swerve. But instead of a declaration of love, Peter began crooning "Some Enchanted Evening," the song from *South Pacific* he'd performed in high school, in his warbly but heartfelt baritone.

A rush of pent-up air gushed out of Josh's chest, and he sagged against the seat in relief. He opened his eyes and watched Peter continue his off-pitch pledge of love to JoJo, who was watching him with a warm-hearted smirk, with one eye on the road. She obviously didn't want Peter to get too carried away with his performance.

When he finished with an operatic flourish, he looked into the rearview to check Josh's reaction. "Now do you remember?"

"I remember," Josh said, his pulse finally returned to normal. "But I suppose JoJo's opinion will be the true test."

Peter looked across at her with overdone eagerness. "So...what do you think?" he said, waggling his eyebrows. "Are you bursting with love?"

She reached over and mussed his hair playfully. "*Bursting*'s an appropriate word for a side-splitting performance like you just gave."

"Thanks, thanks a lot," Peter said, ducking his head grumpily. "See if I ever sing to you again."

"See if I ever complain," JoJo shot back.

They continued to banter back and forth, ignoring the passenger in the back seat. Josh looked out the window with a mixture of relief and heightened anxiety, knowing this had only been a reprieve. Somehow, he sensed he felt more nervous than Peter himself about what was still to come.

And as for JoJo, and what Peter had planned for her, it was clear she didn't have a clue.

Twelve

"What's that?" Grandma Lattimore yelled across the living room.

"Wow, it's a muffler!" Peter held the multicolored knit scarf up enthusiastically for the whole room to see, then turned to his mother. "Thank you, Mom."

She flashed a loving smile down on her son. "I made it larger for you this year." Mrs. Lattimore never seemed to grasp the concept that sons ever physically stopped growing. In her mind, "the boys" just seemed to get bigger and bigger. By the time Peter reached middle age, she would probably be knitting him mufflers the size of Lake Michigan.

Christmas morning with Peter's family was a shock to JoJo. Her own family's custom was to dole out presents as fast as possible and then open them all at once in an explosion of paper and ribbon and gifts. Her brother, mother, stepfather and whatever other relatives happened to drop by would all talk at once, thanking each other over the noise of ripping paper and the sounds of the radio station playing corny holiday music.

This was not the way with the Lattimores.

Peter's family sat in a wide circle all around the living room, everyone dressed in their holiday best. Even the little babies and toddlers wore velvet overalls and scratchy crinoline-lined dresses, waiting expectantly for the presents to be given out to them in an orderly fashion. The Mormon Tabernacle Choir sang softly in the background while adults

sipped coffee and watched as, one by one, every person
opened a gift. Then, once that person had oohed and aahed
to everyone else's satisfaction and explained what it was to
Grandma Lattimore, the next person could open his or her
gift.

According to Peter, they had always done it this way; in
the beginning, JoJo had even found it endearing. But the
beginning had been over an hour and a half ago. This was
going to take forever!

JoJo looked around nervously at Peter's brothers and
sisters, nieces and nephews, none of whom seemed to mind
the leisurely pace of this ritual, which was driving *her* nuts.
How could those little kids not want to tear into their
brightly colored packages, which she knew contained stuff
she would have died for when she was their age. How could
the adults not be itching to know what their spouses had
bought them? How could they all stand to be the focus of
attention of the entire room as they opened their gifts?

That part really made her nervous. What if she opened
something truly ghastly? She was petrified of giggling at the
wrong moment, or having her too-expressive face show
anything but the same abject gratefulness and joy that everyone showed when they opened presents.

So far her worries had been unjustified. This was her first
Christmas at someone else's house, and Peter's family had
gone all out to welcome her. They had given her perfume
and clothes, and she'd even got a bracelet from his mom—
more stuff than she'd ever received for Christmas in her life.
In fact, it was all a little bit overwhelming, considering the
fact that she was only Peter's girlfriend. Somehow she felt
as if she didn't really deserve all the kindness that was being directed at her.

She couldn't help thinking that at least part of the reason
for her discomfort was the fact that she had almost cheated
on Peter. What would his family think about that? Worse,

she'd never worked up the nerve to tell him. But every time she looked at him or one of his family, she was sure they could see the truth in her eyes.

The little kids across the room were just now opening their presents, and Peter leaned over and touched her knee. "It'll be a while before the present loop makes it back to you, if you feel like getting yourself some more coffee," he suggested.

She looked at her half-full cup. "I'm okay," she said.

"Are you sure?" he asked, seeming unduly concerned that she wasn't getting enough caffeine. Was he afraid she was going to fall asleep before the gift unwrapping was over?

Would it ever *be* over?

"I'm fine," she insisted bravely.

Peter's mother shot her a worried glance. "Why don't you go to the kitchen and check on Marcy?" Mrs. Lattimore told her. "She went in a half hour ago and hasn't been back."

"Yeah, she missed her turn!" Peter's sister Ellen said, as if this were a federal offense.

Not sure whether she was being expelled from the living room or sent on an important family mission, JoJo got up and took her coffee cup and Peter's to the kitchen. When she crossed the threshold, she gasped at the sight of Marcy, who was slumped in a chair with her face down on the kitchen table.

She rushed forward. "Marcy, are you all right?"

Before she reached the table, the young woman's head snapped up and she ran a hand wearily through her blond permed hair. "Is it over yet?" she asked.

JoJo laughed conspiratorially. "Not yet. Everyone's concerned that you missed a round of presents, though. Are you okay?"

Marcy picked up her own cup and saucer and brought it over to the counter to pour some more coffee from the monstrous-size thermos Mrs. Lattimore kept well filled for family occasions. "I feel just dandy," she said, "considering that I haven't slept for over a week."

JoJo frowned sympathetically. "The baby?"

Marcy rolled her eyes. "And to think, this is just the beginning. Ben is great—we switch off nights. Unfortunately, last night was my turn." She rubbed her back and stretched. "Now I've got gift fatigue. I'm glad it was you and not one of the family who caught me snoozing."

The offhand words struck JoJo like a light slap in the face. Just what she needed—one more reminder that she wasn't family, that she didn't really belong. Where did she belong? she wondered as she busied herself emptying half a sweetener packet into her cup and the other half into Peter's. When was her life finally going to take root?

Marcy obviously sensed her words had struck a wrong note, but hit upon the wrong reason why. "I mean, this is a great family and everything."

JoJo nodded energetically. "Great family."

"But sometimes it's almost too close-knit," Marcy said in a low voice. "They're so bound up in old routines that sometimes it looks as if they're bored with each other, you know what I mean?"

"Yeah, I do," JoJo said, a glint of understanding beginning to dawn.

"I mean, I love every last one of them—even Ellen, who gives me a hard time—but sometimes you just get tired of a family and its quirks. Or, in this case, lack of them."

"Sometimes it's like that with individual people, too, I guess." *But that didn't mean it was time to just give up on them.*

"Of course it is," Marcy said. "Wait 'til you're married. It seems that half the time Ben and I are either boring each other to tears or making each other madder than spit." She laughed. "Sounds great, doesn't it?"

"Sounds like Ellen talking."

"For all her grousing about marriage, Ellen has some good advice to dole out on the subject." Marcy winked. "She ought to—she's had more practice than the rest of us."

"More practice than me, that's for sure," JoJo said, trying to keep the self-pity out of her voice. In the holiday intimacy of the Lattimore kitchen, she was tempted to tell Marcy that she was having a hard enough time just keeping a dating relationship with Peter together.

Marcy tapped her on the arm. "Peter's a great guy. It'll work out for you two someday."

JoJo worked up a half smile. "Sure, it will," she said, trying to sound optimistic.

There was a light rapping at the kitchen door, and Marcy walked over to open it. Standing out on the porch, which had recently been shoveled clear of snow, stood Josh. He looked hesitantly inside, smiling when he saw JoJo. "Are they still at it?"

The two women laughed. For the first time in weeks, JoJo was glad to see Josh. Another nonfamily person was a welcome change. "C'mon in," she urged.

He stepped inside and Marcy led him to the Lattimore thermos. "You can join us for the final round of gift-giving tedium," she said.

They took their coffee cups and went back into the living room, where everyone, surprisingly, was already standing. The Lattimores were completely out of formation. They turned from where they had been milling about the couch and greeted Josh warmly.

"You're just in time, pal!" Peter said, then, after yelling a reintroduction of Josh to his grandmother, he suggested they all get back to the important business of gifts.

When JoJo moved to sit down, however, she found a huge box resting next to Peter on the couch where she had been sitting, which is what all the attention of the room had been focused on. Peter took her arm and pulled her over to stand beside him.

"This is from me," he said, gesturing toward the box. His cheeks were red, as though he'd been running up and down stairs, which he probably had been to retrieve the box from its hiding place.

She stopped in midstep, scoping out the big present. Where had it come from? The family was likewise amazed by the size of the package, and had stopped their normal orderly activity to inspect it.

"For heaven's sake, Peter," Ellen said, "what did you get JoJo this year—an oven?"

Everyone in the room laughed—the box was about the right size for a large appliance. Tracy gave JoJo an eager shove. "Go ahead, open it."

JoJo laughed nervously. "I'm a little afraid."

"Why?" asked Peter.

"Because anything that big will never fit in my apartment."

"I promise you," Peter said, "this present may just convince you to move out of that apartment of yours."

That remark pushed her curiosity over the edge. JoJo stepped forward, admiring the great wrapping job. Had Peter done this himself? The shiny silver paper had holly leaves printed on it, so that it rivaled even the Lattimores' huge Christmas tree in brightness and festivity. JoJo looked quickly from one family member to the next, certain one of them must know what was inside the box, but none of their faces revealed anything but curiosity.

Except Peter's, of course. He was practically hopping from one foot to the other in anticipation. Josh stood next to him, looking intently at the box, as if those blue eyes could pierce through all that wrapping and cardboard to see what the contents were.

"For heaven's sake, girl," Grandma Lattimore cried in exasperation, "open the cockamamy present!"

Finally she clasped her hand around the thick red velvety ribbon and tugged, untying the massive bow. Then, attempting to accomplish the task with Lattimore restraint, she began tearing the paper off. When she finally got the box open, she pulled tissue paper out until she came to a brightly wrapped box that was perhaps the size a computer would come in. But it was too light to hold a computer.

"Oh, no...." she moaned. The family laughed when they realized she'd fallen victim to an old gag. "Peter, you didn't!"

He looked at her innocently. "Didn't what?"

Next to him, Josh looked a little sick. He was pale, and a thin film of sweat had gathered above his eyebrows. What was the matter with him? Did he know something she didn't?

Restraint became impossible. She ripped into the next box, only to find an even smaller one, and then a smaller one inside that, and on and on. It was too annoying. The boxes decreased in size until finally all that was left was a tiny little white box with a jeweler's name written across it in silver letters. And when she removed the cover, there was only a little velvet ring box left.

She looked nervously at Peter. He was biting his lip, waiting for her to open it. Josh's mouth was set tensely in a ruler-straight line. The room was silent.

"Go ahead," Peter said, his voice a hoarse whisper.

With trembling fingers she pushed on the upper half of the little ring box, until its lid snapped open efficiently, revealing a sparkling green stone surrounded by two clumps of tiny diamonds, set in gold. JoJo's jaw dropped in astonishment as the family members around her let out a collected gasp of surprise.

"Oh, my word!" JoJo heard Mrs. Lattimore exclaim.

"Lord, have mercy!" Grandma cried.

And JoJo knew why. Even with her slim knowledge of jewelry, she knew that rock had to be an emerald, and therefore, the ring must have cost a mint.

Quickly she snapped the box shut again and closed her sweaty palm around it in a fist. She looked beseechingly to Peter. What was he doing? Was this just a gift, or—

He stepped forward and took her hand in his. At first she thought he was just trying to hold her hand to calm her down, but then she felt him prying her fingers away from the box. He got the box away from her, took out the ring and clasped her left hand.

Oh, no, oh, no, oh, no! Not here, she thought—not with all of these people watching. What would she say? She still had a lie on her conscience. Butterflies fluttered in her stomach and her face felt as though it were on fire. She had stepped onto bare stages before in front of hundreds of people and never felt as nervous as she did right now.

She didn't, couldn't, look at him, but she thought fleetingly of Josh. Guilt flooded her. Of all the times for him to have come over—of all the people in the world, he was the last she'd want witnessing this. She felt petrified with discomfort.

And yet, as she looked into Peter's determined yet soft adorable brown eyes, the stampede going on in her stomach slowly calmed, the trembling sensation that seemed to come from deep in her bones eventually stilled and the people around them, rather than seeming intimidating, seeped into her consciousness like the walls of a cocoon.

Peter took a breath and smiled reassuringly at her. "I love you, Jo, and I've never wanted anything so much in my life as for you to marry me," he said straightforwardly. Then, tightening his grip on her hand, he asked, "Will you?"

Her heart thumped loudly in her chest, so loudly she couldn't concentrate on anything else for a moment. The silence around them was deafening, until a familiar voice broke through it.

"What the hell's the matter?" Grandma Lattimore cried. "Is the poor girl in shock?"

"Jo?" Peter asked, his face tensing the longer her silence stretched.

All her thoughts narrowed in on his handsome face, and how directionless, how empty, the prospect of a life without him had seemed to her. Suddenly, all her doubts of the past weeks shed around her like a neurotic layer she was gladly rid of, and she knew what her answer would be, without a doubt.

What else could it be? She had hoped for a miracle to bring Peter back to her, and he had created one himself. He hadn't given up on her. He never would.

"Yes!" she cried, her voice cracking with joy and relief. "Of course!"

Peter's face broke into the biggest, most wonderful smile she had ever seen, and it seemed to her the entire room let out a collective sigh. He slid the ring onto her finger and placed a long kiss on her lips.

When he pulled back, JoJo opened her mouth to speak, but in the next moment, she found herself crushed by jubilant Lattimores. Peter's mother gave her the biggest hug and a wet pink-lipsticked kiss on the cheek, exclaiming and crying all the while about how happy and surprised she was. The sisters hugged her, too, and her left hand became communal property as everyone inspected the ring for herself. Grandma Lattimore was especially interested in eyeballing the piece of jewelry.

"Fancy," she finally declared approvingly.

"I knew that little brother of mine had something up his sleeve!" Ellen exclaimed. "Though I don't know why he couldn't have confided in me. It's not as if I would have told anyone."

"Oh, except the entire town," Tracy shot back over her shoulder, darting a glance at her brother. "But I would have thought he could have told *me.*"

"Even I didn't know," Mrs. Lattimore said, "and I'm the one who's been saving those boxes he used to wrap the ring in in my attic all these years!"

While Grandma, Mrs. Lattimore and the sisters commanded all of JoJo's attention, Peter seemed to retreat farther and farther away into his own circle of handshaking, back-slapping male congratulations. In a few moments, JoJo sensed, the two groups would shift, and the men would all swarm on her and the sisters would harangue Peter for a detailed account of the thought processes that led up to the surprise proposal. Predictable, caring and insatiably content. She smiled. She might be able to get the hang of being a Lattimore after all.

Out of the corner of her eye she saw someone ducking into the kitchen and glanced over to see who it was. Josh turned, smiled at her and sent her a thumbs-up before retreating back to his house next door. She looked for a moment at the empty doorway he had passed through, until her attention was once again reclaimed.

Marcy, fully awake now, gave her a quick hug. "I can tell you're going to shake this family all up."

The small group quieted and Ellen asked, "How so?"

"Didn't anybody notice?" Marcy asked with a devilish little smile and a wink for her would-be in-law. "JoJo had us begging her to open that box and it wasn't her turn yet!"

"Alone at last!" Peter exclaimed as the side door latched shut behind them. It was almost dark, and they had bundled up against the cold, but they walked arm in arm. "Where should we go?" he asked JoJo.

"Somewhere where there are no people," she suggested. "That little park down the street."

They were almost to the sidewalk when Barb poked her head out of her doorway. "Wait just a minute, you two!" she cried. "Where are you going?"

"To neck in the park," Peter said matter-of-factly.

Barb cackled with delight and hopped through the snow to them. "Before you go, I want to see it!"

There was no question what "it" referred to. JoJo ripped off her glove and with a practiced flourish presented her finger for inspection.

Barb let out a pleased gasp. "Beautiful!" Then she hugged both of them. "How wonderful—I'm thrilled for you both," she said in a throaty yet heartfelt voice. "Josh is, too."

"Where is Josh?" Peter asked, although JoJo shot him a look that said they didn't need three to celebrate on this particular occasion.

"An old girlfriend called. He's out painting the town red in your honor," Barb said, then crossed her arms over her chest and shivered. She was wearing only slacks and an angora sweater. "I've got to go inside and get warm!"

Luckily, JoJo and Peter had each other to keep warm. They strolled arm in arm in the park, stopping in every dimly lit secluded spot for leisurely kisses and words that they couldn't speak in front of others.

"I can't wait to get back to Chicago now," Peter said as they collapsed together on a bench.

"Tired of your family already?" JoJo asked, resting her head against his chest.

"Tired of sleeping on the couch." Whenever they stayed together at the Lattimores, JoJo got Peter's room while he was assigned the couch. "Normally it's a drag, but tonight it's gonna be unbearable."

JoJo laughed. "I know what you mean."

Peter kissed her again, then pulled back and looked at her, his expression serious. "For a minute there today I thought you were going to say no."

"I *was* surprised," she said evasively, trying to conceal her grimace. "Especially since . . ."

"Since I'm the most fantastic man in the world and you thought my proposing was too good to be true?" He lifted his eyebrows hopefully.

She smiled. "Okay, you guessed it."

They kissed again, and JoJo wondered if Peter wanted to know whether she really had almost said no. Actually, it had never entered her mind to refuse, only how soon she should say yes, and whether they needed to talk before committing to something so monumental as 'til-death-do-us-part.

"I guess I was surprised because sometimes during the past months it seemed as though you'd lost interest in me," she said, deciding it wasn't too late to talk. And to confess.

Peter frowned. "I have been wrapped up in work a lot lately, but I'm trying to be more spontaneous."

"That's not the problem," JoJo said. "I don't need to be surprised, Peter. I just don't want to be ignored."

"All those months I was working, trying to get promoted, I thought you knew it was because I wanted us to have money, so we could get married and all that."

"You should have told me what you were up to," she said. "I would have been thrilled."

"Are you thrilled now?"

"Yes!"

It was impossible to keep a meaningful conversation going when all you wanted to do was kiss the person you were talking to. They paused to snuggle for a bit longer, then finally came up for air.

JoJo still felt uneasy. She'd been straightforward with Peter about how she'd felt about how he'd acted these past weeks. But what about her own behavior? Would Peter feel so crazy in love with her if he knew she'd come a hairbreadth away from betraying him? If she was going to explain about what had happened with Josh, it was now or never.

She looked into Peter's warm, loving eyes. He was so understanding, and above all, he valued honesty. He didn't believe in the healing powers of little white lies and strategic evasiveness. And maybe he was right.

"Peter..." she began, her voice betraying her nervousness with a wary quiver.

"Hmm?" His eyes closed, and he nuzzled her hair comfortingly.

"There's something I have to tell you."

Peter sighed. "Is it important?"

"Very." Probably, these would be the most important words she ever said to him. They might even make or break their engagement.

He looked at her with his devastating brown eyes and her breath caught in her throat.

Was she crazy? Why risk losing the thing that made her so happy—again? It was bad enough that she'd almost had an affair with his best friend; to tell Peter now, weeks after it *hadn't* happened, would be completely stupid. Worse than stupid. She would be throwing away all that she loved with both hands.

Nobody liked the truth that much, no matter what Peter said.

"JoJo?" he asked, worried by her silence.

Maybe someday, when she was an old, bored married Lattimore lady, she would look back on the way Josh had treated her and be thankful. Probably there would be plenty of times in the coming years when she would be attracted to some guy she was working with, or would meet a guy who would flirt with her because he hadn't noticed her wedding ring. But Josh had taught her that the love she wanted was more than mere flattery—it was the deep lasting commitment that she was going to share with Peter. Forever.

And to keep that kind of commitment fresh for the next fifty years or so was going to take vigilance—starting now. She straightened up and linked her hands behind Peter's neck.

"You were going to tell me something important," he coaxed. "What was it?"

"Just the same thing you'll be hearing from me for the next several decades," JoJo said with more happiness than she would have guessed one person could contain. "I love you, Peter Lattimore."

*   *   *   *   *

Next month,
don't miss Tammy's story in

Getting a Clue: Tammy

by Wendy Mass

One

Tammy gathered her long, light brown hair away from her face and let it fall behind her back. She was trying to ignore that it was eighty-five degrees in her tiny cubicle and that her shirt was sticking to her in a *very* unprofessional way.

The lace bra Kyle had given her last Valentine's Day was clearly visible through her white cotton T-shirt, and she was glad most people had left for the day.

She smiled to herself, picturing Kyle slouching around Victoria's Secret, his green eyes focused on the floor and his face red with embarrassment. He'd sworn he would never go in there without her again.

She glanced at the new watch her parents had given her last month for graduation. Almost 5:30. She would give Mr. Willoughby ten more minutes to assign her a new story, otherwise she would have to run Matrons Of Champaign-Urbana Plant Marigolds On University Avenue! as next week's headline. She was grateful she had been able to turn her senior-year internship into a summer job, but the weekly *Urbana Tribune* wasn't exactly transforming her into Tammy Shelman, Top Investigative Reporter. At least it *was* allowing her to stay in town with Kyle, who still had two more years of school left, and for that she would even put up with writing a story about Mr. Willoughby's dog, Mitzi.

She opened her notebook and reread the notes she had written during yesterday's particularly boring staff meeting. She bet no one else's notes turned their lives into a miniseries!

72 TROY DRIVE—THE SUMMER MONTHS

STARRING **TAMMY SHELMAN** AS HERSELF

SUPPORTING CAST, in order of appearance:

Kyle Clarke: Incredibly Handsome Frat-Jock Boy-friend of Tammy, His Mother Thinks He Walks on Water, Roommate of Jack

Jack Vinick: Loyal Friend and Roommate of Kyle, Gentle Giant and Current Boyfriend of Maggie

Maggie Preston: Pixie Poet and Long-Distance Run-ner, Sorority Sister of Tammy, Girlfriend of Jack, Roommate of Rose

MINOR CHARACTERS, ladies first

Rose Tannen: Roommate of Maggie, Sweet Girl-Next-Door

Mitch Sommers: Serious and Shy Premed Student

"Are you still here, Tammy?" a guy's voice asked.

Tammy whirled around, startled. It was Michael, her favorite reporter. She looked down at her watch: 5:40 p.m.

"Not anymore I'm not," she said, gathering her things.

Michael glanced at Tammy's nearly see-through T-shirt and quickly looked away. She smiled at his discomfort, liking him even more for it. He had graduated from the University of Illinois also, but about five years ago.

"Shouldn't you be getting home to Hayley?" she teased, as they headed for the parking lot.

He nodded. "She said she's planning something special, but won't tell me what it is."

"Maybe she's going to propose!"

"Yeah, right," he said. "She's waiting for that diamond ring, but I don't know if I'm ready yet."

Tammy didn't know what to say, since they had never spoken this openly before. She stood there awkwardly, and he said goodbye and turned the corner.

She shrugged and hopped in her little red economy car, turning on the cassette player with one quick move. The air-conditioning was set on high and she could hear her dad's voice saying things like, "Drains the battery," and "Guzzles gas."

Responding to some long-ago embedded Jewish guilt, she turned it down to low and turned the new Tori Amos tape Maggie had lent her up to high. She passed Kyle's fraternity house and noticed the top floor was gutted already. If it hadn't been declared a health hazard, Kyle would be living there, instead of with her. Since he could charm the pants off anyone with one of his famous grins, she was glad he wouldn't be surrounded by the frat party scene all summer. Speaking of charming someone's pants off, she was hoping for a quiet, romantic evening to take her mind off the heat wave and put it back on the great summer they planned together.

As she pulled up to the curb in front of the house, she could hear the music blaring. it sounded like—but no, it couldn't be. The Village People! Someone was playing "Y.M.C.A." Visions of her quiet night with Kyle evaporated.

The door opened as she reached the porch and Kyle stepped out to hug her.

"My little working woman, home from the office!" He squeezed her tight and she returned the embrace. He was tanned from his part-time job doing general maintenance around campus, and was his usual cheery self. She looked over his shoulder into the house and didn't even *recognize* some of the people.

"So much for having the house to ourselves," Tammy said, stepping inside. There were beer cans everywhere and the house looked messier than usual.

"Well," Kyle began, trying to look sheepish but not succeeding. "I invited a couple of the guys from Campus Construction to come over, and you know how news spreads."

She did. The party grapevine traveled faster than the speed of light. She watched Jack and three other boys doing the "Y.M.C.A." dance and laughed in spite of herself. At six foot one, Jack towered above the other guys. He and Maggie, who was only five-two, made an odd couple.

Kyle plopped down on the couch and motioned for Tammy to join him. She sighed and sat down on the arm of the nearly threadbare couch that had come with the house. She wanted to tell him about her day at work and how Mr. Willoughby had given the assignment she wanted to this girl Josie with big boobs, but she could tell he wouldn't be interested. Well, maybe Josie's boobs would pique his interest, but then once he realized they were peripheral to the story, she would lose him again.

"So how was work, Tam?" Kyle asked, raising his voice above the music.

"Fine. Nothing special," she answered, deciding it wasn't worth talking about. She reached over and pushed some hair away from his eyes. He grabbed onto her arm and swung her onto the couch with him. Then he glanced appreciatively at her still-damp T-shirt and kissed her neck. This brought whistles from the "Y.M.C.A." dancers, and Maggie called out, "Get a room!" with her usual impish grin. Her short blond hair twirled around her face as she danced across the crowded room. She always looked like she was having the most fun of anyone, even though she almost never drank. Her father was an alcoholic, so Maggie forced herself to avoid the temptation.

Tammy laughed as Maggie twirled in front by the couch and she pretended to push Kyle away.

"Wanna fool around?" he whispered.

She pretended to be shocked. "Not with all these people in the house!"

"I'll get rid of them," Kyle said, holding on to Tammy's shoulder as he stood up on the couch. He reached behind him, snagged a half-empty beer from Jack and took a swig. "Okay, everyone," he announced loudly. "The party's over. Go home."

"We are home," Maggie and Rose yelled.

"All right, you can stay," Kyle agreed. "And you, and you," he added, pointing to Jack and Mitch. "And definitely you," he said, patting Tammy on the head.

"Gee, thanks," Tammy answered. She noticed people really were leaving. Kyle had this way of making people listen to him, even if he was kicking them out of a party.

"I'm going upstairs while you guys clean up the damage," she announced, grabbing her shoulder bag. She heard everyone groan and was glad she hadn't been around to contribute to the mess.

She and Mitch were the only ones with their own rooms, and she loved hers. She shared a bathroom with Rose and Maggie and they all agreed the old-fashioned bathtub with feet was the best part of the house.

When they had moved in last month, Maggie had given her a funky tie-dyed tapestry to hang on her wall for atmosphere. Rose had decorated their room in a fit of Laura Ashley and the tapestry clashed terribly.

Maggie had whimpered quietly when she first saw all the pink furniture Rose's mother had given her, but firmly put her foot down when Rose suggested they paint the walls pink to match. Maggie often hung out in Tammy's room, saying she felt more at home with the tapestry and Tammy's large candle collection. Kyle joked about getting her a lava lamp to complete the "sixties throwback look," and Tammy was embarrassed to admit she wanted one.

She closed the door, peeled off her T-shirt and turned on the plastic fan, which whirred into action. She stood in front of it and closed her eyes, loving the feel of the cool breeze. After a minute she turned around and held up her hair so the breeze was on the back of her neck. She pictured Kyle in his navy tank top and tan shorts and she slowly opened her eyes and focused. Kyle was standing not two feet away in the doorway, just watching her and grinning.

She wanted to say something, to ask how he had come in so quietly, but she didn't really care. She loved being surprised. And she loved Kyle. He pushed the door closed and put his strong arms around her, squeezing tight. They started kissing and he ran his hands lightly up and down her bare back. She reached up and held tight to his shoulders, pushing her breasts hard against his chest. Without separating, they shuffled over to Tammy's single bed and Kyle lay her down gently underneath him. She traced the muscles on his arms and noted that the heat wave had definitely not hampered his sex drive. He began pushing down the straps of her bra and Tammy knew he was going to start kissing her breasts. Before Kyle, she hadn't let anyone do that. In fact, she hadn't done too much of *anything* before Kyle, and she was glad he had been her first, even though she knew he had slept with a few girls before her.

She felt his breath on the thin lace and she arched up to him. Right as his mouth landed, there was a knock on the door.

"The Chinese food is here!" Jack yelled. "Come and get it before it's gone!"

Tammy and Kyle stared at each other.

"Bummer," Kyle said.

"Do you think they'll save us any if we don't go down?" Tammy asked, her heart still racing.

"What do *you* think?"

"You're right," she said. "Let's go."

"Not like that, I hope," Kyle said, gesturing to her nearly naked chest.

Tammy scrambled off the bed and grabbed her favorite U. of I. T-shirt from the drawer. She turned away from Kyle, took her bra the rest of the way off and quickly slipped the shirt over her head. She changed into her favorite pair of faded jean shorts and fluffed her hair a little in the mirror. For some reason she had always felt shy standing naked in front of Kyle; it made her feel as if she were on display. Kyle had told her that made no sense, but after going out with her for over a year and a half, he had finally given up trying to understand her weirdness.

They got downstairs in time to sample some food from each carton. Only the housemates were there, and they had cleaned up pretty well. The Village People had mercifully transformed into Enya, and Tammy thought her haunting voice was perfect for a hot summer night.

Kneeling around the coffee table, no one spoke as they stuffed themselves with cashew chicken, egg rolls, moo-shoo beef and steamed veggies. When Tammy couldn't eat another bite, she leaned against the couch and said, "Who's up for Pictionary?"

The three guys groaned and rolled their eyes.

"Again?" Mitch asked. "Don't you ever get sick of it?" Since he was premed, all his drawings resembled people's insides. His team usually lost.

"It's okay, Mitch," Tammy said, reaching under the couch, where she had stashed the game last week. "Kyle can play with Rose and I'll be on your team—then maybe you'll have a chance. I won a drawing contest in second grade, you know."

"You tell us that every time we play," Kyle pointed out as Tammy and Maggie set up the notepads and the timer.

"Did I tell you the picture was of my cat, Muffin, carrying an umbrella?" Tammy asked.

Kyle laughed. "You had a cat named Muffin? What a stupid name."

"Hey, I've killed for less than that. Muffin was a prince among cats. A constant joy, a—"

"Okay," Kyle said, holding up his hand. "We get it. Muffin rules the heavens above."

"That's better. Now let's roll to see who goes first."

Jack won and picked a card. Tammy flipped the timer, and Jack began scribbling.

"A cow!" Maggie yelled. "A house! No...Zeus?"

Jack looked at her in amazement. "Zeus?"

"A tree?" Maggie asked meekly.

"No talking," Kyle said.

Mitch and Tammy started humming the "Jeopardy" tune as time was running out.

Jack kept scribbling and pointing to the paper. He looked at his girlfriend with exasperation.

Maggie picked up the paper and turned it upside down. "Is it a telephone?"

"Time!" Tammy and Rose and Kyle yelled joyously.

"It's so obvious." Jack sighed, taking the drawing from Maggie. "It's a gopher. See the paws and the teeth?"

"What paws?" Maggie asked. "I'm sticking with Zeus."

"It's our turn," Tammy said, picking a card. She flipped the timer herself and hunched over the paper.

Four seconds later she was done. Mitch leaned over the table.

"A garden hose?"

"Yes!"

"Oh, sure," Jack said. "I get a gopher, a living, breathing intricate member of the animal kingdom, and she gets a garden hose. Does that seem fair?"

"Cheer up, honey," Maggie said, patting him on the arm. "She's an old lady. She needs her fun."

Tammy sometimes forgot that everyone else still had two years of college left. She was jealous that they didn't have to face the real world yet.

"Just hope you look as good as she does at that age," Kyle said to Maggie.

Tammy snuggled up next to him. "My hero," she said, resting her head on his shoulder.

The phone rang and it was Kyle's mother. Thus the game officially ended—they had learned by now that Lila Clarke was not short on words.

Tammy left Kyle to his phone call and followed Maggie up to her room. Maggie and Rose were both taking summer classes and books were scattered all over the floor.

"How's your class going?" Tammy asked, picking up a book of poetry called *Dancing with the Lights On*.

"It's great so far," Maggie answered, settling into Rose's pink rocking chair. "The teacher is so cool. She grew up in this big family out in the desert of New Mexico. Her parents were artists and her poetry is totally bizarre, all about spirituality and sex."

"This *is* a sociology class, right?" Tammy asked.

"The teacher says that poetry is a uniting force between cultures, and by studying it, we learn more about ourselves."

Kyle ducked his head into the room.

"That was a short call," Tammy kidded. "Your mother must not be herself tonight."

"She had to run—C.J. was having her crisis of the week."

"Hey, I love your sister. She's always been very nice to me."

"That's because you're as crazy as she is," Kyle said.

Tammy threw Maggie's stuffed bear at him. He moved away and the bear landed unceremoniously on its head.

"Hey," Maggie said, "don't get Puddleglum in the middle of this."

"Why can't you name your teddy bear something normal like other girls?" Kyle asked. "What's wrong with Snuggles, or Fluffy, or, dare I say it, Muffin?"

Maggie bent down and gently picked her bear up off the floor. "For your information, Puddleglum is a character in a very famous book. Perhaps you've been hit on the head with too many baseballs to remember it."

"Hey, I'm going to bring the Champaign-Urbana Cougars to the world series of Little League this summer," Kyle bragged. "But I didn't come up here so you two could bask in my glory. I wanted to tell Tammy that Ray's having people over and I have to go."

Ray was Kyle's "big brother" in the fraternity, and when Ray called, Kyle jumped. Ray wasn't such a bad guy—he just took Kyle away from her more than she would have liked.

"Jack's coming, too," he added. "You know, just the guys this time."

"We'll just sit here and read poetry, won't we, Mag?"

"We sure will," Maggie agreed. "So rush along to your childish games—we'll be exploring the inner workings of the human soul."

He gave Tammy a kiss on the cheek and left.

Tammy lay down on Rose's bed and absentmindedly pulled little threads from the pink-and-white comforter. "Mag?"

"Yeah?" Maggie answered, not looking up from her poetry book.

"Do you think men were created to drive women crazy?"

"Show me some men first, and I'll let you know."

Tammy laughed. Sometimes it was pretty hard to think of Kyle as a man. But at two o'clock in the morning, when he climbed into bed with her and pulled her close to him, there wasn't a doubt in her mind.

The Loop™

Hey! If you've missed any LOOP titles,
then here's your chance to order them:

#20201	GETTING IT TOGETHER: CJ by Wendy Corsi Staub	$3.50 U.S. ☐	$3.99 CAN. ☐
#20202	GETTING IT RIGHT: JESSICA by Carla Cassidy	$3.50 U.S. ☐	$3.99 CAN. ☐
#20203	GETTING REAL: CHRISTOPHER by Kathryn Jensen	$3.50 U.S. ☐	$3.99 CAN. ☐
#20204	GETTING PERSONAL: BECKY by Janet Quin Harkin	$3.50 U.S. ☐	$3.99 CAN. ☐
#20205	GETTING ATTACHED: CJ by Wendy Corsi Staub	$3.50 U.S. ☐	$3.99 CAN. ☐
#20206	GETTING A LIFE: MARISSA by Kathryn Jensen	$3.50 U.S. ☐	$3.99 CAN. ☐
#20207	GETTING OUT: EMILY by ArLynn Presser	$3.50 U.S. ☐	$3.99 CAN. ☐

(limited quantities available on certain titles)

TOTAL AMOUNT	$
POSTAGE & HANDLING	$
($1.00 for one book, 50¢ for each additional)	
APPLICABLE TAXES*	$ _____
TOTAL PAYABLE	$ _____
(check or money order—please do not send cash)	

To order, complete this form and send it, along with a check or money
order for the total above, payable to Silhouette Books, to: **In the U.S.:**
3010 Walden Avenue, P.O. Box 9077, Buffalo, NY 14269-9077;
In Canada: P.O. Box 636, Fort Erie, Ontario, L2A 5X3.

Name: _____

Address: _____ City: _____

State/Prov.: _____ Zip/Postal Code: _____

*New York residents remit applicable sales taxes.
 Canadian residents remit applicable federal and provincial taxes.

▼ Silhouette®

LOOPBL6

MONTANA ™
Mavericks

Stories that capture living and loving beneath the Big Sky, where legends live on...and mystery lingers.

This March, meet an unlikely couple in

THE LAW IS NO LADY
by Helen R. Myers

Why would an honorable court judge want to marry a disreputable outlaw? Was it because she loved the child he sought custody of, or had she simply fallen for a rugged loner who could give her nothing but his name?

Don't miss a minute of the loving as the passion continues with:

FATHER FOUND
by Laurie Paige (April)

BABY WANTED
by Cathie Linz (May)

MAN WITH A PAST
by Celeste Hamilton (June)

COWBOY COP
by Rachel Lee (July)

Only from ▼ *Silhouette*® where passion lives.
™

MAV8

Get Ready to be Swept Away by
Silhouette's Spring Collection

Abduction *&* Seduction

These passion-filled stories explore both the dangerous
desires of men and the seductive powers of women.
Written by three of our most celebrated authors, they are
sure to capture your hearts.

Diana Palmer
Brings us a spin-off of her Long, Tall Texans series

Joan Johnston
Crafts a beguiling Western romance

Rebecca Brandewyne
New York Times bestselling author
makes a smashing contemporary debut

Available in March at your favorite retail outlet.

ABSED

Silhouette celebrates motherhood in May with...

Debbie Macomber
Jill Marie Landis
Gina Ferris Wilkins

in

Three Mothers & a Cradle

Join three award-winning authors in this
beautiful collection you'll treasure forever.
The same antique, hand-crafted cradle
connects these three heartwarming romances,
which celebrate the joys and excitement of
motherhood. Makes the perfect gift for yourself
or a loved one!

A special celebration of love,

Only from

Silhouette®
TM

—where passion lives.

MD95

Enter the world of

Spine-tingling romances
from the dark side of love.

In March, enjoy this Silhouette Shadows title:

SS #50 THE WOMAN IN WHITE
by Jane Toombs

One look into Guy Russell's eyes and Lia Courtois
knew their togetherness was destiny. Guy, too,
felt the hypnotic lure. But Guy's hidden past and
Lia's fragile future hinged precariously upon the
mysterious woman in white!

**One chilling, thrilling love story each and
every month...from Silhouette Shadows.**

Available in March at a store near you.

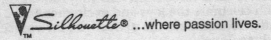 ...where passion lives.

SS395-R

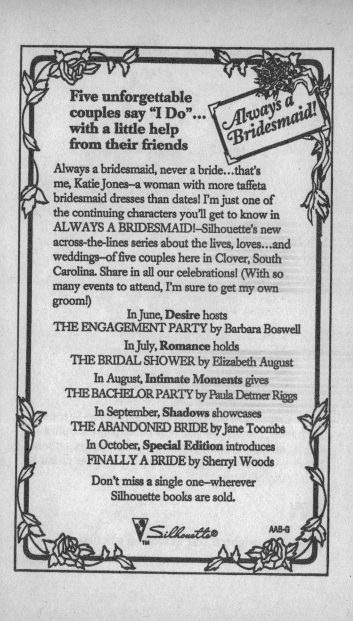

Five unforgettable couples say "I Do"... with a little help from their friends

Always a Bridesmaid!

Always a bridesmaid, never a bride...that's me, Katie Jones—a woman with more taffeta bridesmaid dresses than dates! I'm just one of the continuing characters you'll get to know in ALWAYS A BRIDESMAID!—Silhouette's new across-the-lines series about the lives, loves...and weddings—of five couples here in Clover, South Carolina. Share in all our celebrations! (With so many events to attend, I'm sure to get my own groom!)

In June, **Desire** hosts
THE ENGAGEMENT PARTY by Barbara Boswell

In July, **Romance** holds
THE BRIDAL SHOWER by Elizabeth August

In August, **Intimate Moments** gives
THE BACHELOR PARTY by Paula Detmer Riggs

In September, **Shadows** showcases
THE ABANDONED BRIDE by Jane Toombs

In October, **Special Edition** introduces
FINALLY A BRIDE by Sherryl Woods

Don't miss a single one—wherever Silhouette books are sold.

Silhouette®
™

AAB-G

New York Times Bestselling Author

Who can you trust when your life's on the line?
Find out this March in

Stevie Corbett is in jeopardy of losing everything—her career,
her future…her life. Her fate rests on keeping the truth a
secret, but there is one reporter who already knows too much.
She could lose everything…including her heart. All he has to
do is betray her trust.…

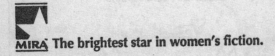

MIRA The brightest star in women's fiction.

MSBTOV